CW01650036

Reg: 1880–1901

Reg: 1880–1901

Alastair Nairn

The Pentland Press Limited
Edinburgh • Cambridge • Durham • USA

First published in 2000 by
The Pentland Press Ltd.
1 Hutton Close
South Church
Bishop Auckland
Durham

British Library Cataloguing in Publication Data.
A Catalogue record for this book is available
from the British Library.

ISBN 1 85821 822 5

Typeset by CBS, Martlesham Heath, Ipswich, Suffolk
Printed and bound by Antony Rowe Ltd., Chippenham

Chapter 1

He was born in 1880, the fourth child of his parents, Colonel and Mrs Win-Wantock. His only brother, Arthur, was eight years older than him, and his two sisters, Olga and Mary, were six and four years his senior. When he was very small his sisters adored having this little baby to play with. He spent his early years almost entirely in female company: his mother, his nanny, his sisters and their governess. His father took little interest in his sons until they approached prep-school age. However, Reg proved to be a good scholar and under the capable Miss Brown, his sisters' governess, was above average when the time came for him to go to his prep-school. Athletically, he had done little other than ride a rather fat pony along with his sisters.

The Wantock Estate was quite large, some 1,500 acres. All the farms were tenanted except the home farm which was managed by the estate agent. The Colonel's interests, since he retired from the army, were local government, politics, shooting and fishing, along with many social engagements which his wife adored.

By the time Reg was two, Arthur was already ten and beginning to be included in some of his parents' activities. On shooting days he was allowed to join the beaters and on occasions his father would take him with him on fishing trips. Once at his prep-school Arthur was promoted to feed in the dining-room except for dinner.

He had his supper with Mrs Bell the housekeeper in her sitting room. This arrangement continued until he left his public school. Mrs Bell was a wonderful woman who adored the young gentlemen. When Arthur had school friends to stay she would entertain them royally at her supper table and they all loved her. On the other hand she was a clever disciplinarian and insisted on good manners, while enjoying a good joke. The result was that the boys respected her and never took advantage of her.

The girls gravitated from the nursery to the schoolroom from where they did not emerge until they were fourteen. They were then promoted to dining-room meals except for dinner. They had supper in the schoolroom.

When the day came for Reg to go to school the task of kitting him out was delegated to Mrs Bell and Nanny. Mrs Bell, who had no experience of buying boys' clothes, took advice from Arthur and so Reg was supplied with all the appropriate clothes and saved the indignity of arriving at school improperly equipped.

When the day came he hated leaving Nanny and his other female companions. Along with his mother he was driven to the station in a carriage. This was exciting as he had never been in a train before. The train journey was not long and a short cab trip took them to the school. He was introduced to the headmaster and then handed over to Matron and that was the last he saw of his mother until the next holidays. Matron took him round the school, showing him the common room, the classrooms, the changing room and which his locker was. Then they went upstairs and he was shown his dormitory and his bed. They returned to the common room where he was introduced to several small boys, one of whom was detailed to take him to tea when the bell rang.

So this was school. He sat and listened to what the other boys were saying but didn't understand the half of it. By doing as he was told by the others or just following them he got through the rest of the day, but he did feel lonely as there was no Nanny to run to.

Next morning the five new boys were set a test and he did so well he was placed in the second bottom form. Slowly he began to find his feet. The masters were very strict in class but out of class he found them quite nice. In the dormitories the beds were set round the walls and in the centre there were tables with a basin and a mug for each boy and a towel. Beside each bed there was a chair and there was a 'po' underneath.

At seven each morning a hand bell was rung. The handyman then entered with a huge jug and proceeded to put a little tepid water into each basin and mug. They then washed their faces, cleaned their teeth and got dressed. They left their pyjamas on their unmade beds. Who emptied the pots and basins and made the beds was not known. When the next bell sounded they proceeded downstairs and filed into the dining-room with the smallest boys leading.

The boys sat at long tables on benches and the food was brought to them; there was no choice, they either ate it or left it. When they had finished they went to the common room and there was a period during which they were supposed to go to the loo. Life was controlled by that hand bell.

The games were organised by the masters and as it was the winter time it was football. Reg quite enjoyed running around after the ball but he was never any good at it.

And so the days and weeks went by and end of term came. He had of course written his weekly letter home which he found very difficult with nothing to say. He usually received a letter from home which was very often written by Nanny and not his mother.

He once had a letter from each sister which were all included in one envelope.

Finally, they were taken to the station by horse bus and put on the train for home. On arrival at his station he was met by the coachman and driven home. He arrived there quite determined to cut loose from the nursery and become a real man, or at least a boy. His hopes in this respect were rudely dashed when he was informed that he was to eat in the schoolroom and not the dining-room as Arthur had done on going to school. Arthur was at home with a friend but they were both sixteen and could not be bothered with an eight year old.

Once Reg had had his breakfast with his sisters he took to going out for walks by himself. He knew most of the paths and lanes through the estate as he had walked them with Nanny. On one occasion he landed up at the under-keeper's cottage. There he found Tom, the keeper's son, who was just his age. On going up to him he noticed that he had something in his arms.

'What's that?'

'It's my ferret, Jenny.'

'Can I hold it?'

'Well, if it doesn't know you it might bite you.'

'Can I stroke it, then?'

'Oh, yes, that's all right.'

'What are you waiting for, Tom?'

'I am waiting for Dad coming home and then we are going to go and check the snares?'

'Can I come too?'

'You will have to ask Dad.'

As he said that a black labrador came bounding up.

'I will put Jenny away,' Tom said, when he saw his father approaching.

'Hello, Master Reg, what are you doing here, just back from school?'

'Yes, I was wondering if I could come with you and Tom to the snares.'

'Yes, I suppose so; does the Lady, I mean your mother, know you are here?'

'No, she doesn't mind anyway.'

John Drew who was under-keeper to his father and had grown up on the estate, said, 'We had better get going,' and he chucked the empty pheasant feed bag into the shed and picked up his game bag. As they walked down a path through the wood John said, 'Well, how do you like school, Master Reg?'

'Oh, it's all right, but this is much better.

They emerged into a grass field and proceeded along the fence side. They had not gone far before Reg saw a rabbit lying flat to the ground and he wondered why it did not run away. John walked straight up to it and seizing it by the small of the back in his powerful hand, lifted it up and removing the snare wire from round its neck, he broke its neck by a quick twist of his hand and popped it into his game bag. Reg watched carefully as Tom reset the snare. The next time Reg asked Tom to show him how to set the snare, and so began his education into game keepering. After a few more snares had been cleared, John pulled his big watch from his pocket and, glancing at it, said, 'I think it is time you were going back for your lunch, Master Reg.'

'Must I?'

'Yes, I think so, do you know the way from here?'

Reg, who had not been paying much attention to where they had gone, looked around and was obviously not too sure.

'Tom, you take him down and put him on the path that goes through the rhoddies; he will find his way all right from there.'

The two boys went off together and when they parted Reg asked if he could come another day.

'Yes, of course, that is if I am not at school,' and they parted.

Reg ran all the way home as he did not wish to be late for schoolroom lunch. As he had no watch he did not know what time it was. As he ran he thought to himself, if I am late they might stop me going out by myself. All was well but his sisters said, 'Where have you been all morning with those muddy boots?'

'Oh, I was helping John to clear his snares.'

'Doing what?' they asked again, so he gave the same reply, finishing with, 'you won't tell anyone, will you?'

At that moment Miss Brown returned and they had lunch.

Some time after lunch Miss Brown took the girls out for their walk, but that was not for Reg. He went through to the front of the house and knocked on the door of his father's study. 'Come in,' he heard, so in he went.

'Hello, Reg, what do you want?'

'Oh, I was wondering if I could look at some of the books in the library.'

His father got up and, walking over to him, put his hand on his shoulder and said, 'Yes, which ones do you want to look at?'

'The bird ones and the shooting ones, please.'

As they arrived in the big room with its shelves of books his father said, 'What were you doing this morning, didn't I see you running up from the rhoddies just before lunch?'

'Yes, I had been out with John and Tom helping to lift the snares.'

'Did your mother or Nanny know that you had been out doing that by yourself?'

'No, I didn't think they would have liked it. Is it all right if I go again?'

'Yes, certainly. Let's have a look for some of these books.'

They spent all afternoon together looking at books and discussing pheasants, partridges and all sorts of other birds.

Eventually his father said, 'It must be your tea time, you had better go back. If you wish to go out with John and Tom you just go but don't tell me. I will not tell anyone I know you are going; we will keep that a secret.'

That night he went to bed a very happy boy; things were certainly looking up. From that day on his relationship with his father changed. He no longer was frightened of him, but of course he still respected him.

One afternoon a few days later Reg was just about to leave the house when he ran into his brother Arthur waiting in the hall with his gun.

'Where are you off to, Reg?'

'Oh, I don't know, just somewhere.'

'Would you like to come with Bob and me, we are going to try to get a pigeon.'

'Yes, that would be fun. Is that gun heavy?' asked Reg.

'No, not very, it's only a 20 bore.'

'What does that mean?'

'Well, it is smaller than Father's which is a 12 bore. Come on, then, and you just stay with me and don't talk and all will be well.'

The three of them soon arrived at a large plantation and Arthur placed Bob under a large oak tree into which the pigeons flighted before dropping down onto their night perches. Arthur and Reg moved on to a similar position at the other end of the wood. The evening proved too still and very few shots were fired, most of the birds spotting the gun before he could get a shot. However, Arthur did get three and Bob one. It was not long before it got too dark so they collected the birds and set off for home. Reg found himself carrying three of the birds. He really was growing up.

On the way home Arthur asked Reg if he was coming to the shoot on Saturday. 'If you would like to come, I suggest you ask Drew or John if you could join the beaters.'

'Yes, I will do that.'

When Reg finally arrived back in the schoolroom for tea the girls had just about finished.

'Where on earth have you been this time, don't you know when tea time is?'

'Oh, I have been out shooting pigeons with Arthur and Bob.'

'Well,' said Miss Brown, slightly deflated, 'make sharp and finish your tea.'

Next morning, as soon as he had finished his breakfast, Reg was off to find John. It was further to his house than to his father's but he had got to know him well so that was that. He found Tom and asked him if he was going to be a beater on Saturday.

'Oh, yes, I expect I shall be made a stop which can be very boring, but sometimes you see interesting things. One day a fox came and looked at me for quite a long time. That was fun.'

When John arrived he said, 'That would be all right. Be at my father's house by nine o'clock and you had better have a mackintosh and waterproof over-trousers, as the kale will be very wet.'

When he got home he went straight to Nanny and announced that he was going beating on Saturday and would need his mackintosh and waterproof over-trousers. 'Have I got any?'

'No, of course not.'

On that he left the room rather crestfallen. After some thought he decided to go and talk to his father about it. He called him

Father now; he was too grown up for Daddy. His father was most helpful and told him just to go to Drew's house without over-trousers.

On Saturday morning he rushed through his breakfast and was soon on his way to Drew's house. Drew handed him over to John who was to be in charge of the beaters. Tom was there too so that was perfect. Everybody seemed to have a stick so he picked one up for himself. They did not have far to go for the start of the first drive and he was placed on John's right and Tom on his left. Once John had heard the whistle signal to start he gave the signal and they all started. Nobody spoke but they all tapped the trees with their sticks and beat any thickets on their line. After a few minutes he heard a pheasant rise and someone shouted, 'Over'; then after a short pause he heard a shot. As they got further and further through the cover he heard more and more shots. Reg could not see the guns until he was almost through and then he saw his father shoot one bird and then a second one before the first one struck the ground. It was all most exciting.

The next drive finished almost in the same place but came from a different direction. At the flushing point there was a strip of trees which led off to one side. Reg and Tom were left there with strict instructions to keep tapping a tree but not to talk. Their job was to stop any birds escaping up the strip. Reg and Tom had been placed about twenty-five yards apart with a bush in between them. Reg, from where he was, could see two of the guns. The boys were standing there tapping away with their sticks when suddenly there appeared a roebuck. When it saw Reg it stopped in its tracks and stood gazing at him just a yard or two away. He hadn't been told what to do if a roe appeared so he just stared back at it. Suddenly, there was a tap from Tom and the buck dashed past him and jumping gracefully over the fence made a dash for it between the guns. Nobody fired at it as his father liked the roe and did not allow them to be shot.

Nanny had his lunch ready for him and he could not stop talking about all he had seen, and then he was off again for the afternoon.

The garden cart with its driver had followed round and the game bags were emptied into it after each drive. At the finish of the last drive all the game was emptied out and laid in rows for the official count of the day's bag. Reg thought he heard Drew tell his father that there were 154 pheasants, 6 hares and 2 pigeons. When he got back he was too late for schoolroom tea so Nanny gave him tea. That night he was quite happy to go to bed early.

Christmas came and went and amongst his most treasured presents were a pocket knife from Arthur and a bird book from his parents. The rest of the holidays soon went by with visits to Tom where he got quite friendly with Jenny the ferret, and visits to the farm where he helped Nan to feed the chickens and with milking the cows. In the evenings he spent a lot of time in the library and studying his new bird book.

These holidays had made great changes in his life. He seemed to know his father better, he had made friends with Tom, John, and Nan and he felt much more independent. However, he was still very much a loner and enjoyed his quiet evenings in the library by himself.

Soon it was time to go back to school. He was sorry to go but there was no question of tears. Things began to go better this term. He was still doing well at his lessons and he had started to learn drawing which he much enjoyed, but the big difference was he now had manly things to talk about with the other boys.

Soon after term began a boy got measles and was put in the 'San'. Reg wasn't too sure what that meant and he hoped he would not catch it. His hopes were dashed when one day he began to feel miserable, cold and shivery. He went to Matron who diagnosed measles. He was told to go and fetch his pyjamas and so on and he could bring a book if he wished. The San was just a special dormitory, separate from the others. He was put into bed and his temperature was taken. He was told he must not get out of bed without permission. He felt so miserable and there was no Nanny to go to, so he was more than happy to stay in bed. A few days of misery were followed by about a week of convalescence before he was allowed back to school. By the end of term the other boys had given up calling him a 'sissie'. He had learnt to play draughts and one of the older boys in his class was teaching him to play chess, and soon another term was past and he was on his way home again.

He was met at the station by the under coachman, Sam Siltoe. Sam was only in his twenties and they enjoyed one another's company. 'We don't see you about the stables, Master Reg, don't you like the horses?'

'I don't know; I have only ridden that fat Rose and she is not much fun.'

'Why don't you have a word with your father and ask him if you could have a ride on Silver, your father's hack? You could go with my mate Len.'

Len was the under groom. The grooms looked after the riding horses and the coachmen the driving horses. Time passed quickly and soon they were home. He spent the rest of that day catching up with everybody from his parents to Nanny. His mother thought that he looked pale and thin. She said, 'I will talk to Nanny and see if we can get you looking fitter.'

'I'm all right.' He did not wish to be stopped going out to see Tom.

Next morning was very wet so he had to put off going to see

Tom. At breakfast he asked Mary if she could play chess. 'No.'

'Can you play, Miss Brown?'

'No, I am afraid I can't.'

'I think there is chess in the cupboard in the billiard room,' Reg said. 'I will go and ask Father if we can have them, then I will teach you, Mary.'

'All right,' said Mary, rather hoping that he did not find the chess set.

Reg dashed off to find his father. 'What do you know about chess?' his father asked.

'Oh, a boy has been teaching me at school.'

'I will play a game with you and see how much you have learnt.' His father had played quite a lot years ago while he was in the army.

'I will go and tell Mary that you are going to play; I don't think she was very keen to learn anyway.'

Father found his son a very good pupil and soon they were having very good games together.

Next morning the weather was better and he set off to find Tom. When he got to the house there was no sign of Tom but he found John washing out the kennel. John told him that Tom's term did not finish till the end of the week.

'What are you going to do when you have finished that?' Reg asked.

'I will be going to look to some of my catching pens.'

'What are catching pens?'

'You come with me and I will show you.'

'Good,' and soon they were on their way. As they walked John explained to Reg that each spring they caught hen pheasants and put them in a pen with one or two cocks and collected the eggs when they started to lay.

'Why do you do that?'

'Well, as we collect the eggs we put a dozen under a broodie hen and she hatches them out, then we let the hen pheasant go and she makes her own nest and that way we get more young birds.'

As they came over a little bank Reg saw a small wire cage with two hen pheasants in it. Once they got up to it John showed Reg the conical wire tube through which the birds found their way in but could not find the way out. Later Reg would learn how to make all these ingenious traps. John lifted a small door on the top of the cage and quickly caught the two hens. He carried them over to a big pen, it must have been about 25 yards square with sides six feet high and a big mesh net over the top. He opened the door and let the hens go.

'Why don't you make that catching tube go straight into this cage?'

'That's a very good question, Master Reg, and I will tell you why. If Mr Fox comes along he could get into the pen, but now he can only get into that little cage and at most would only get one or two birds. If he got in here he could not only kill more birds but he could eat all the eggs as well.'

Reg had a lovely morning with John who chased him off home in time for lunch. That afternoon he wandered up to the stables where he found Rug, the head groom. All the heads, the head groom, the head coachman, the head gardener and the head keepers were known by their surnames and all others by their Christian names.

'Hello, Master Reg, we don't often see you in the stables.'

'No, but Sam said I might be able to ride Silver. Do you think that would be all right?'

'Of course it would; we would welcome one of the young

gentlemen riding exercise with us. Mr Arthur, he doesn't take much interest in the horses, do he? Before you could ride Silver you would have to ask your father. When you have done that you let me know and I will take you myself the first time.'

His father was delighted when he asked if he could ride Silver and that started him off on another new ploy. That evening Reg sent a message to Rug that he would be riding next morning at nine o'clock. When he arrived at the stables next morning Rug was waiting for him.

'I take it, Master Reg, that you want to learn all about the horses, what goes on in stables and all that sort of thing, not just how to ride.'

This statement took Reg by surprise as he had not thought about that side of it. 'Yes,' he said, rather hesitantly.

'Come along, then,' and he was led off into the harness-room. It was a large room, very clean and tidy. There seemed to be harness hanging on every wall. One side all appeared to be brown and the other side black. Rug pointed to the brown and said, 'This is all our stuff, the black is the carriage stuff. We will just have a quick look round before we take Silver's tack out.'

Reg was shown first the bridles and bits, then the stirrups and leathers and finally the saddles. Rug then lifted a bridle down from the wall and handed it to Reg.

'You take that and I will bring the rest.'

They found Silver in the end stall; the others were full of carriage horses. Rug put the saddle on a saddle rack on the back wall and then led Reg up alongside Silver. He removed her head collar and, taking the bridle from Reg, showed him how to put it on. That done, he fetched the saddle and showed him how to fit and secure it.

'Now, you take hold of the reins and push her back out of the stall and lead her out into the yard.'

Reg found that he hardly had to do any pushing; Silver just did it herself. Once in the yard he was shown how to mount. It was a bit of a struggle and he needed a little help. Rug then fetched old Bob, who was already saddled, and off they rode together. As they rode Rug gave Reg all sorts of advice on riding and on what to do on various occasions. They rode for about forty minutes, both walking and trotting. They did not canter or gallop. Once back, Reg dismounted and was told to take Silver into her stall while Rug put Bob away. Silver walked into her stall automatically and Reg stood there beside her, wondering what to do next.

After what seemed quite a long time Rug appeared and said, 'Sorry, Master Reg, I just stripped off Bob's things and put them in the tack room.'

Reg was then shown how to undo the girths and remove the saddle and finally how to remove the bridle and put on the head collar.

'That will do for today; we will deal with grooming and cleaning the tack another day. I hope you enjoyed your ride.'

'Oh, yes, but there seems an awful lot to learn.'

'Not too much really, Sir, you will soon pick it up. When can I expect you again?'

'Tomorrow, if that's all right,' so that was fixed. As he walked back to the house he realised how much more comfortable riding Silver was than that fat old pony.

The Easter holidays soon went by, his time being divided between riding, exploring the woods with Tom and playing chess with his father. As his legs got stronger Rug took him further and they started to canter as well. He also enjoyed learning about feeding, grooming and looking after the tack.

His exploits with Tom included visits to the hens to see the little pheasant chicks which had started to hatch, looking for bird's nests and identifying what bird they belonged to. Quite often they had to refer to John for identification.

My readers must not think that because they are seldom mentioned, Reg had little contact with other members of his family. He fed in the schoolroom and of course told his sisters of his exploits, but they were not really interested just as he was not interested in their pursuits. His relationship with his mother and with Arthur were much the same.

Back at school Reg enjoyed the summer term. In school he looked like coming out top of his form at the end of his first year. Cricket was 'all right' but he was not much good at it. As the school was in the country the boys were allowed to roam within prescribed limits and he and a few kindred spirits spent much time doing that. They found the odd bird's nest and on one occasion they found a family of little hedgehogs. There was not much to report that term except sports day, to which, to his great surprise, his father and mother came. He was not involved in the final of any event so he was able to spend the time with his parents showing them round the school and so on. He loved having his parents there like so many other boys. After all, they did not live very far away, not like some boys whose parents were in India. Towards the end of July he was on his way home again and once again he was met at the station by Sam. This time, as they drove home, they had lots to talk about after all his experience in the stables.

After his round of the household he did not rush off to the stables or to see Tom but to the garden to see if there were any strawberries left. He sought out Mr Green the head gardener and asked him.

'Oh yes, Master Reg, were you looking for some?

'Well, yes, could I have a few, we never get them at school.'

'You know, Master Reg, I am not supposed to give you fruit from the garden but as you are just back from school you just go and pick a few but don't tell any one I said you could.'

Having eaten a few he went back to thank Mr Green, and found him debudding chrysanthemums.

'What are you doing?'

Mr Green explained to him that by removing these buds the main flower would grow much bigger. He watched for a few minutes and then said, 'I must go or I will be late.'

'Nice to see you, Master Reg; will I be seeing you again? We see your sisters from time to time but we never see you.'

'I will come and see you again. I want to know how to grow things.'

'I will look forward to that,' and they parted.

That evening Mrs Bell produced strawberries for supper as a special welcome home, but this time he had cream and sugar as well.

He did not ride this holidays as all the riding horses, except for Silver, were out to grass. He divided his time between Tom and the woods, the farm and the garden. He never thought that the garden would be such fun. Mr Green was very patient and explained all about the plants which had to be grown each year and those which overwintered and came up again the following year, and so began what became a lifelong interest.

The highlight of the holidays was the two-week visit of his cousin Peter Plumb. Peter's mother was Reg's mother's youngest sister; she had married a lawyer and they lived in London. Peter was the eldest of five children; next to him came two sisters followed by a brother and a baby sister. Reg went with Sam to meet Peter at the station. Peter was two months older than Reg but he was not a country boy. This gave Reg an opportunity to show off and he became much bolder in so doing. He took Peter to see the young pheasants and walked him miles through the woods. On one occasion Reg tore a large hole in the seat of his trousers while playing on the farm. On another occasion Peter climbed on to the edge of the large water trough in the yard while trying to reach a sparrows' nest. He slipped and splash! sat down in the trough. When these things happened Nanny was always very cross but she never exposed them to Reg's parents.

When the visit came to an end, a tentative plan was made for a return visit in the Christmas holidays. Life slipped back into its familiar pattern of school and holidays.

At school he continued to do well at his lessons and remained in a form above his age group. One thing which pleased him was to beat the boy who had taught him to play chess. At home he was growing up fast. He could now ride the hunters. It was not long before another summer term had come round. At the end of this term there was to be a major change. Arthur was to leave school and go to the Royal Military College, to prepare to join his father's old regiment. Arthur, aged eighteen, was now a real man; he used to go away to stay with friends for dances and shooting parties.

Reg was now into his eleventh year and was becoming more and more fascinated with the garden, He had planted seeds in the spring and could not wait for the next holidays to see how they were growing. Before he knew where he was it was almost a year since Arthur had left school.

One day that summer term Reg received a very unexpected letter from Olga. It was a long letter telling him that she was going to join a family in Paris, and that Mummy was going to take her to London to get some grown-up clothes. 'Then she is going to take me to Paris herself. It's all so exciting. I think I shall have gone before you come home for the holidays, that's why I am writing to tell you.'

Reg could not see that this would make much difference to him. He and Olga were good friends but they never did much together.

It had been arranged that Reg would join Peter and his family for the first week of their holiday in Cornwall. It was all quite exciting. Reg was to go by train by himself. He was instructed that he was to leave his train at a certain station and join the London train when it came through and that he would find Peter and his family on that train. All went well and he found them without difficulty. The family were in two compartments; Mr Plumb, Peter and the two elder girls were in one and Mrs Plumb, Nanny and the two small children in the other. They spent the rest of the journey playing all sorts of games most of which were initiated by Mr Plumb. Reg thought he was very nice. In the hotel the party had four bedrooms. Mr and Mrs Plumb were in one, Peter and Reg in one, Norah and Pru in another and Nanny and the two small ones in the fourth. As it was quite late by the time they arrived the small ones went straight to bed and had their supper upstairs, but the four elder children joined the parents in the dining-room for supper. Once they had fed, the girls were sent off to bed.

Aunt May spent the next few minutes questioning Reg about his life at home and then it was time for the boys to go to bed. As they went along the passage Peter said, 'Let's go and say goodnight to the girls.' He burst into their room without knocking and there standing quite naked was Norah combing her hair. Peter seized her round the waist and pulled her onto the bed and started tickling her.

'Don't do that, Peter, you know I don't like being tickled.'

'All right,' Peter replied and they both stood up.

Reg just stood and stared. He had never seen a naked girl, girls to him were a sort of mystery whom you almost did not touch. Peter and Norah had shared a room, however, since they were two and four years of age. Reg's attitude towards girls began to change from that time on; he found them rather fun to play with.

The week went quickly. Uncle Robert took the boys sea fishing one day which was great fun. In fact the whole week was very relaxed, so unlike home. When his time came to an end he was quite sorry to leave, he was getting on so well with everybody including the girls. The journey home was uneventful but seemed to take an awful long time by himself.

Back at home with Olga away and Miss Brown on holiday Mary was at a loose end. Although she was four years older than Reg she began going out with him; she particularly enjoyed the visits to the garden. Here they found something which they both enjoyed.

There now occurred something which brought them even closer together. Nanny left. Nanny, who had been with the family since Arthur was born, decided that if she did not move now she would soon be too old to start again. This move left a huge void in the lives of both children and they turned to one another to fill part of it. A housemaid was detailed to look after their domestic requirements but she, of course, wasn't the sympathetic solver of all problems Nanny had been. Mary had Miss Brown to go to but she did not understand boys' problems. Reg found himself going to his father and sometimes to his mother and even to the butler for advice.

Reg took Mary all over the place, in the woods and on the farm. Mary, who was more down to earth than her sister, enjoyed this life and learnt a lot about country and animal life. Soon the holidays were over and it was time to return to school.

During the term Reg received two letters from Mary. The first one was chiefly about how dull it was only having Miss Brown all day, not even Nanny. The second contained the exciting news that she had a letter from Olga saying she was coming home for Christmas together with all sorts of other news. The only other thing of note that term was his acquisition of a catapult which he received in return for helping a boy with extra work.

When he arrived home for the Christmas holidays there was an air of great excitement everywhere. His chief source of information was Mary. From her he learnt that Olga would arrive in two days accompanied by a girl friend and then there was to be a house party, a shoot and a dance about New Year. All this sounded pretty dreadful; the shoot wasn't too bad but the rest was just boring. Mary finished by saying, 'Daddy says that as Mummy is away collecting Olga we are to join him for dinner tonight and that you are to put your best suit on.'

'Where am I to have breakfast and all my other meals?'

'Here, I suppose in the schoolroom.'

At dinner that night his father said to him, 'Reg, I am afraid this is going to be a rather difficult holiday for you. Olga has a girl friend coming home with her and Arthur is coming home for Christmas and is then being joined by two other young officers for the shoot on the 28th. Mary is old enough to join all the festivities but I don't think they would amuse you. I suggest you speak to Mrs Bell and arrange to have your meals with her; that will give you much more freedom.'

'All right I will,' but he thought it was going to be a very dull holiday.

During the course of the evening he learnt that the dance was to be on Old Year's Night and that there were some others coming to stay. He had never experienced this sort of activity before and in some ways it was quite exciting.

He had sent a message up to the stables that he wished to ride next morning so after breakfast he rushed up there. Rug was delighted to see him. During the course of their ride they visited Tom. He was not there but Reg left a message with his mother that he would be up to see him soon but owing to the goings on at home he could not say when. He lunched with his father and Mary and joined the reception party who were awaiting the return of the young ladies from Paris.

It was after three o'clock when the carriage drew up. His mother, of course, alighted first followed by the two girls. They were so smart, with neat close fitting bonnets, high waisted long coats, buttoned boots and muffs. Mary ran to greet first her mother, then Olga who greeted her with, 'This is Penny; she comes from Australia so she is going to spend the holidays with us.'

'Hello, Penny, have you been in England before?'

'Yes, on my way to Paris I spent nearly a month with my grandmother in Sussex.'

'I hope you like it here.'

'I am sure I shall, I know it will be great fun.'

Reg, who had greeted his mother, was slinking away when he heard Olga's voice, 'Reg, aren't you going to say how-do-you-do to Penny?'

He stopped and, turning, approached Penny rather shyly with his hand out. Penny squatted down, took his hand and gave him a kiss. Holding on to his hand she said, 'I have heard a lot about you, you will be able to show me all sorts of things I ought to know.'

'I can't think what.'

'Oh, about pheasants and gardens,' and they walked into the house together. Once inside they all dispersed to find their rooms and Reg escaped. He found his way to the library and sat down. He had never been kissed by a girl before; it was only his mother and Nanny who gave him a kiss. He rather liked Penny, she seemed different to his sisters, and he began to wonder what he could do with her and where he could take her. He sat there a long time, sometimes reading, and sometimes just daydreaming.

Suddenly, the door burst open and the three girls entered. Olga was showing Penny round the house. They were talking so hard they did not immediately notice Reg. Turning, Penny saw him.

'Hello, Reg, what are you doing?'

'Oh, just reading.'

'Can I see what you are reading?' and she moved over to him. 'Reg, will you sit next me at dinner tonight, I want to talk to you.'

'I can't, I don't go to dinner, I have my supper with Mrs Bell.'

'What a pity; I wanted to make a plan with you, for tomorrow. Can't we make a plan now?'

'Come on, Penny,' interjected Olga.

'Wait a minute; I am making a plan with Reg.'

They decided to meet in the front hall next morning dressed for walking.

The next day Reg was in the hall in good time and when Penny appeared she was dressed in some of Olga's old clothes.

'Good morning, Reg, what are you going to do with me today?'

'Well, I thought you might like to see the horses and then we could walk through the wood and go and see Tom. Tom is my friend, he is the son of the under keeper, you would like him.'

As they left the house Reg dived straight in: what's Australia like, how long does it take to get there? and more. Penny started to reply and Reg was so fascinated he did not want to reach the stables, but of course they did.

'Good morning, Master Reg, got a young lady with you today.'

'Yes, can we see the horses?'

'Of course you may, you know where they all stand; just be quiet and don't frighten them.'

Reg took her first to the carriage horses, then to the hacks and finished with the hunters. He showed her all the ones he had ridden. They went to the tack room, the harness room and the carriage house. Penny was amazed at the variety, but even more at the orderliness and tidiness. It was so unlike home where the horses lived out in the paddocks and were just pulled in when you required them. As they were about to leave they ran into Rug.

'Are you coming for a ride with Master Reg?'

'Yes, but this is so different to home.'

'If I may enquire, Miss, where is home?'

'Oh, I live in Australia.' This led to a long conversation, and Reg began to wonder if they would have time to go and see Tom. Before they left they had made a tentative plan to ride next morning and that Penny would ride astride. She had never ridden side-saddle.

They took a path through the wood which passed quite close to a fox earth, then the pheasant breeding pens and many other causes for diversion. When they arrived Mrs Drew said, 'Do you know the time, Master Reg; you will have to bustle if you are not going to be late for lunch.'

'Thank you, tell Tom I will see him another day, Happy Christmas,' and off they went.

They were both somewhat out of breath as they came through the front door and ran straight into Father.

'You will have to hurry if you are not going to be late.'

'Oh, Mrs Bell won't mind.'

'Tell Mrs Bell that you will have all your meals with us except dinner, starting from today.'

'Yes Sir.'

After lunch Reg cleared it with his father that it would be all right for Penny to go riding with him the next day. Rug would come too.

That evening Penny arranged to borrow some riding clothes from Olga. Arthur arrived home in time for dinner and was delighted to find Penny was a member of the house party. He had never met Penny before, but any budding young army officer was always glad to meet a new young girl. At breakfast next morning Arthur was surprised to see Penny appear dressed in riding clothes.

'I say, Penny, what are you dressed up like that for?'

'Reg and I are going riding this morning; we fixed it up yesterday.'

In those days every young gentleman could ride, it was the only means of transport except for driving. Arthur, however, had never shown much interest in equestrian sports but since arriving at the RMC he had become quite keen and was beginning to quite fancy himself as a horseman.

'I will come with you, it won't take me a minute to change; there are plenty of horses in the stable.'

Penny called to Reg, 'Is it all right if Arthur comes too?'

'I suppose so,' was the rather reluctant reply; he resented the competition from his elder brother.

They were greeted at the stable with, 'Good morning, Mr Arthur, I wasn't expecting you.'

'I thought I might as well come; could you pop a bridle and saddle on something for me?'

'I won't be a minute, Sir.'

As they waited for Rug, Penny explained that at home she just rode to go with the boys rounding up the cattle or sheep. 'I have never played polo and of course we don't hunt foxes. I know nothing about jumping; some people show jump but we never have.'

A few minutes later they were on their way with Arthur and Penny leading followed by Reg and Rug. As they entered the field where there were a number of small schooling fences. Arthur said to Penny, 'Would you like to have a go at jumping? I tell you what, I will give you a lead and you can follow me.'

They trotted off and Rug turned to Reg and winking, said, 'You wait here with me.'

In a few minutes they came cantering back with Penny following some five lengths behind. The gallant young officer arrived at the fence full of confidence but at the critical moment his mount stuck in his toes and swerving to one side deposited his rider over the fence where he landed on his bottom. Penny drew up at the fence and laughing called out, 'Are you all right? That was a good lead you gave me!'

Arthur stood up and began to make some rather lame excuses. In the presence of a young lady he had to restrain his language.

In the meantime Rug and Reg went to catch the loose horse. As they returned with it, Rug said in a loud voice, 'What about you giving the young lady a lead, Master Reg?'

'Yes, I will; come on, Penny, follow me,' and he cantered off up the field to the next fence. Over he went without a moment's hesitation followed by Penny. They circled round and in front of Arthur and Rug popped over the first fence. Arthur was about to have words with Rug but he thought better of it. On rejoining the others Reg said, 'We are going to ride up and see Tom and make plans for the shoot next week.'

This time it was Arthur and Rug who followed. They found Tom and made their plans for the shoot and then set course for home.

At lunch Penny, who was sitting next her host, said, 'I had my first lesson in jumping this morning. Reg gave me a wonderful lead.'

'Reg, I did not know that you had started jumping.'

'Oh yes, Sir, Rug has given me several lessons.'

Nothing was said about Arthur's mishap.

Next day was Christmas Day and it took two carriages to convey them all to church. After the service there followed a period of chat outside before returning to an enormous lunch. That afternoon the Colonel, accompanied by Reg, walked to the home farm to wish all up there a Happy Christmas; the others went their separate ways. Next evening the staff Christmas supper was to be held. The household were served a light evening meal after which the Colonel, accompanied by his wife and family, went through to the servants' hall. Here were assembled the house staff and estate staff but not the farm staff as that would make too many. After a few minutes chatting the Colonel made a short speech and wished them all a Happy Christmas, then the house party retired.

The following morning Reg and Penny, this time accompanied by Mary, went for a ride. Arthur waited at home to welcome his two friends who were coming for the shoot and were to stay over for the dance. The shoot went well and Reg enjoyed his day with Tom and the beaters. Now that there were three young men in the house Reg felt rather out of it and longed for the dance to be over so things could get back to normal. It wasn't to be a ball as Olga was not 'out' yet; that was to come next summer.

Reg was not interested in the dance so he had his supper with Mrs Bell and slipped off to bed. Once the New Year was over

Arthur and his friends returned to Sandhurst and his mother took Olga and Penny to London to see some theatres before taking them back to Paris.

At home the Colonel made several trips to see tenant farmers. He took Mary and Reg with him. They enjoyed these rides.

Reg enjoyed school. The competition in the classroom was a challenge and he liked the company. The Easter term was short and before long he was home again. This holidays there was plenty to do: the hen pheasants had to be caught, there were horses to ride and in the garden sowing and planting. He also had several good games of chess with his father. His mother was fully occupied preparing for the return of Olga who was to be launched onto the Débutante scene this summer. A town house was taken for the season and by letter and every other way she noised abroad the fact that she and her daughter would be in town for the season. Olga was due to leave Paris at the end of April so her mother went over and together they enjoyed themselves buying all the latest fashions which Olga would require for the season.

Back at school, Reg, owing to his scholastic achievements was in a form with boys about a year older than himself. Many of them were destined to move on to their public schools within the year. The headmaster advised Reg's father that he too should make a similar move at that time. As soon as this decision was made known to Reg he began to discuss it with the other boys. He discovered that there were two other boys going to the same school as he was and one to the same house. David, who was a year older than Reg and much bigger, was a very nice boy, good at games but found his scholastic studies very difficult. Reg got on well with him and they struck up a strong friendship. David's grandfather was an Earl who owned a large estate in Yorkshire and lived in a very large house.

David's father also lived on the estate. David invited Reg to spend part of the summer holidays with him. Reg had no difficulty in obtaining the necessary permission from his father and the boys began making plans. The plan that emerged was for Reg to go for three weeks at the beginning of the holidays but all this was contingent on both boys passing their Common Entrance Exam.

It was arranged that Reg would travel home with David. As they travelled home on the train, Reg learnt that David was one of five children. Unlike Reg, David was the eldest of the family. He had a sister of eleven, one of eight and two brothers aged seven and five.

They were met at the station by David's father who looked much younger than Reg's father. He had been in town to deal with some business. After driving for some ninety minutes they arrived at quite an imposing country house set in an attractive park. The house was large but not as large as Wantock. Reg received a great welcome from Lady Sells and the children. He was the first schoolfriend to be brought home by David.

'Come on, Reg, I will show you our room,' and David started up the stair. It was a large room where they found a housemaid busily unpacking Reg's luggage.

'I have put all your things on this side to keep them separate from Mr David's, I hope that is all right.'

'Yes, thank you.'

David explained that he had only recently been promoted to this room from the nursery floor which was one floor further up. 'This floor is all bedrooms so we will go down.'

This house was a much more symmetrical building than Wantock. The exploration did not take long but it was already getting late.

'We will have to go and change for dinner which is at 7.45.'

They arrived in the drawingroom in good time where they found Lord and Lady Sells enjoying a pre-dinner drink which had been poured for them by the butler. Sharp on time the dinner was announced and they went through to the diningroom. They were just four so it was a very informal party. The conversation, which covered all that had been going on during the term, was confined almost entirely to horses. There were descriptions of races, the births of foals, and much time was devoted to the Earl's racing successes. Reg discovered that his host and hostess were called Emily and Jack but of course he would never think of addressing them like that. Emily asked him all about his home circumstances. Reg explained that he was much the youngest and as such was a bit of a loner. He explained that although he did ride quite a lot his father was more interested in shooting than hunting and that they were not involved in racing. He thought Emily was charming, she seemed so young and was so relaxed and easy to talk to. Just before they were sent off to bed Jack said to his son, 'I expect you will be receiving an invitation from your grandfather to take Reg over to see him.' David got on very well with his grandfather and was a great favourite of his.

Next morning at breakfast the footman came in with a small silver tray on which was a letter. He offered it to David who then asked his father's permission to open it. It was indeed a letter from his grandfather inviting him to take Reg over for lunch tomorrow, Saturday, and stay and watch the cricket match in the afternoon. The local village team played their home matches on the private ground in front of the Mansion. After breakfast David wrote a brief note accepting the invitation.

The family breeding stud was located at the Lodge which was the name of David's home. Once the letter was dispatched David took Reg on a visit to the stud. They were welcomed by the stud groom who proceeded to take them on a long tour of inspection. They were first taken to the paddocks to see the brood mares and foals. David and Bob discussed each one in turn and David proved to have a very good knowledge of the various pedigrees. From there they visited the yearlings. They finished up in the yard where there were one or two two-year-olds who were starting their training. Finally, they were shown the two magnificent stud stallions. Before returning for lunch David arranged for his two ponies to be brought down next morning at 11.30 as they would be riding over to the Mansion.

For Reg, the morning had been both exciting and absorbing. There was so much to see and everything was on such a large scale. Thoroughbred horses were certainly the most beautiful creatures and he longed to learn more about them. Lunch gave him an opportunity to do just that. His host was very kind and patient in answering all his questions. He very much enjoyed being with David's parents; they were both so easy to talk to. In the afternoon they visited the duck pond. It proved to be only some three quarters of a mile away and was situated in a beautiful wooded glade. The pond itself covered less than three acres, and was oval in shape with a stream feeding it one end and flowing out the other end. There was a boat-house with a small boat. David explained that they fished for trout from the boat as it was difficult to fish from the bank owing to the proximity of the trees. On their return journey they visited the garden where they found a few ripe strawberries.

That evening Reg received his first lesson on how to play whist. As they went to bed that night Reg told David that he wanted time next morning to write up his journal. He had never written a diary before but his father had given him one and suggested that this visit would be a good occasion on which to make a start. What he had been given was in fact just a notebook into which he had to make his own entries of dates, etc. Next morning he retired to his room and sat long looking at the first blank page. He eventually decided that he would start when he joined David on the train. Once the start was made things went well and he soon found that it was time to get ready for his trip over to the Mansion.

Just before the half hour David came to collect him, explaining that they must not be late as his grandfather was very fussy about punctuality. They would have to ride quite slowly as the ponies would be soft coming off the grass. The two ponies looked more like two miniature thoroughbreds. They proceeded by a variety of tracks and lanes and emerged directly opposite the most magnificent gate, close by which stood the lodge keeper's house. After some ten minutes they rounded a corner and came into view of the largest house Reg had ever seen. Instead of going to the front door they turned off and rode round the back to the stables. Here they found a groom who took the horses, saying he would see them watered and fed. David said that they would come round for them, probably about 6.15 p.m.

They entered the house by a door at the back and David led the way through what seemed miles of passages to a cloakroom where they left their caps and whips, and washed and brushed up before going through to meet David's grandparents. Passing through a swing door they entered a huge hall out of which there rose the grand staircase. Crossing to the far side David knocked on the study door.

'Come in.'

It was a large room with a big bow window looking out onto a lawn and flower beds. David's grandfather was sitting on a leather-covered armchair reading some papers. When he saw them he got up.

'Oh, it is you, boy, come and sit down.'

'Thank you, Sir, this is Reg who is staying with me. We are at school together, and we are both leaving and going on to the same school.'

Grandfather was a tall man for those days, about 5ft 11ins. He was well covered but not too fat for a man of his age. He had grey hair, a reddish face and a white mustachio. 'Sit down there,' and he pointed to a sofa. They sat and chatted during which Reg was closely questioned about his family and home. After a time the Earl pulled his watch from his pocket by its gold chain and looking at it, said: 'It is time we went through to see if Mother is ready for lunch.'

He always referred to his wife as Mother. Mother was a small round woman with a cheery face and fair hair going grey. She was dressed in a light coloured summer dress which went down to the ground. She approached them saying, 'How nice it is to see you, David; who is this?' and she shook them both by the hand. After David had introduced Reg she said, 'You will be hungry, let's go and find out what we have for lunch.'

They sat at a small round table at one end of a large room. Most of the room was filled by a huge table which must have been able to seat twenty people. They were waited on by a butler and a footman. Conversation slowed as the boys waded through several courses.

As they were about to leave the table the Earl said, 'I hope all our team turn up this afternoon; if not you will have to fill in.'

Reg hoped that only applied to David as he was no cricketer. Lunch finished they went out to see the game started. Fortunately, both teams were at full strength so their services were not required.

They spent a very happy afternoon watching the cricket and chatting to the other spectators.

When they went to say good-bye the Earl said, 'Would you two boys like to come up for the grouse shooting next week? Your father is coming and he could bring you up. There would not be room in the house for you but I am sure Mrs Williams would put you up.'

'Thank you very much, Sir, we would like to do that.'

'Well, I will be in touch with your father about the arrangements.'

Having taken their leave they went off to the stables to find the ponies.

The next morning, Sunday, David and Reg walked to the church with Lord Sells while her Ladyship was driven accompanied by her two daughters. There was a great family reunion after the service with the party from the Mansion. This provided an opportunity to finalise the arrangements for the grouse shoot which was to be on Wednesday and Thursday the 12th and 13th of August. Lord Sells arranged that he would drive up on Tuesday afternoon with the boys, leaving his wife and the rest of the family at home.

The highlight of Monday was a visit to the harvest field. In those days when the corn was cut by a binder drawn by three horses it was the practice to start at the outside of the field and cut round and around. This meant that the area of standing corn got progressively smaller. As this happened all livestock, chiefly rabbits, took refuge in the ever-decreasing area of standing corn. As this moment approached, all available farmhands and children arrived armed with sticks. Finally, as the area got smaller and smaller, rabbits would break out and make a dash for the safety of the hedgerow. They had to run the gauntlet of all the sticks and many did not make it. This was always considered a good way of helping to keep the rabbit population under reasonable control.

The journey up to the moor next day proved to be a very hot one; there was not a cloud in the sky. They stopped at an inn for an hour and a half to rest, water and feed the horses. Meanwhile they too had a very substantial meal. Sometime after five they drew up at a farm.

'This is where you two are to lodge,' David's father announced. He gave the boys strict instructions on how they were to behave and the time they were to be at the big house next morning. By this time Mrs Williams had arrived and they were introduced.

'It is very good of you to put these two lads up; see that they behave and don't spoil them.'

'Oh, it's a pleasure to have the two young gentlemen and I will see that they are up in good time in the morning.' As the carriage drew away Mrs Williams said, 'Come on, boys, pick up your bags and follow me.'

She had already picked up the two biggest ones. They walked up the front path and in the door. Directly in front of them was the staircase. She proceeded straight up and into a room on the right at the top. Putting down the bags she said, 'Well, I am afraid that's all we can offer you.' She showed them the geography of the house and finished up in the bedroom. 'Unpack your bags and when you are ready come down and we will have our tea.'

Neither boy had ever had to do this before; however, they made what they thought was an adequate job and proceeded downstairs. As they entered the parlour they met Mr Williams for the first time. He was sat on a hard wooden chair at one end of the table. He was in his shirt sleeves with his powerful bare arms folded across his chest.

'Come on in, boys, and make yourselves at home; there is a

chair waiting for you,' and he pointed to one on either side of the table. Almost before they were seated Ted, which was Mr Williams' name, started talking. 'You have never sat at the kitchen table before, I'll bet you,' and on and on he went laughing at his own jokes and any reply the boys made.

Mrs Williams had been in domestic service before she married Ted and was accustomed to handling the young gentlemen.

'Come on, Mother, we are all starving.'

'All in good time, did you ever go hungry in this house?'

At that moment she started placing plates of steaming hot soup in front of them. The Williams were both in their late fifties. They had three children, a boy and two girls, all of whom were married.

After a very substantial meal Mother cleared the table and the boys stayed chatting to Ted.

'What happens at a grouse shoot, Mr Williams, we have never been at one?'

'You just call me Ted, everyone just calls me Ted. Anyway, I will tell you about the grouse shoot.'

He explained that there were three ways of shooting grouse: walking up, shooting over dogs and driving. When walking up, the guns formed up in a straight line with keepers with retrievers in between them. They then walked over the moor and shot any birds that got up. Shooting over dogs, which they would do tomorrow, was much the same, but specially trained dogs were used to find the grouse. The dogs were specially trained to range back and forward about twenty-five yards in front of the guns and when they winded grouse they would stop and stand looking at the spot. This was called pointing. When this happened the nearest guns got ready and advanced slowly until the birds got up. Normally there would be only one pointer working at any one time. As this work was very hard work for the dog they were changed at frequent intervals. Driving was very different. The guns stood in a row of butts and the beaters drove the birds over the guns. The boys had a wonderful evening listening to Ted who told them stories of happenings on the moor.

As the clock approached nine Mrs Williams announced, 'It is time for bed; you will have a hard day tomorrow and we have to be about by five thirty to get the cows in and milked before breakfast. I will see you woken in time, have a good sleep,' and she bade them goodnight.

The boys had never enjoyed an evening more. It was all so new to them and Ted's stories had kept them in fits of laughter. Shortly after seven next morning they were woken by a cheery, 'Time to get up, boys, you will get your breakfast after the half hour,' and with a wink she added, 'and mind you leave your rooms tidy; there's no staff here to run after you.'

Having partaken of a very substantial breakfast Mrs Williams checked that they were properly kitted out and sent them on their way to walk to the shooting lodge. They were to be there not later than eight forty five. As they walked they discussed all that Ted had told them the previous evening. They entered the house and immediately ran into the Earl.

'Good morning, boys, I knew Mrs Williams would ensure you were here on time. I am sure you had a good evening, they are such a good couple. David, you come with me and you, Reg, go with Jack.'

'Yes, Sir.'

There were to be six guns shooting that day; two of the guests had stayed in the house overnight; the other two were local.

Soon they heard the Earl announce in a loud voice, 'Come on, it is time we were off,' and he led the way out of the door and up a path through a wood. After about half a mile, as they emerged from the trees they met up with the keepers who were carrying their masters' guns and cartridges. The Earl announced the position of the guns in the line and the plan for the morning. Jack was to be the right hand gun which meant he had quite a walk to get in place.

'Come on, Reg, we have a bit to go.'

Once the line was formed the dog handler released his first dog and the shoot began. Reg was fascinated watching the dog range back and forward across the front of the line as they advanced. Suddenly, the dog stopped and pointed just as Ted said it would. The nearest guns advanced with their guns at the ready. Soon after passing the dog the birds flushed and three were shot. The retrievers then went to work and having picked the birds the shoot continued. The walking pace was very slow to give the dog time to work, which was just as well as it turned into a very hot day.

The lunch stop was very popular, everyone having acquired a good thirst. The lunch had arrived in a pony trap and was served by a footman assisted by the groom. The keepers emptied their game bags and the count was fifteen brace. The boys enjoyed listening to the conversation and answering questions put to them.

During lunch one of the other guns, a Mr Gray, invited Reg to join him for the afternoon, which invitation Reg, having obtained Jack's permission, accepted. Mr Gray, who was probably about Jack's age, was one of those very active little men and was much more chatty than Jack. Whenever there was a pause for the picking of birds he kept asking Reg questions. When the day was over and the bag was being counted he asked Reg if he and David would care to come over to his home for a night next week, saying, 'I will be down your way and could bring you back with me.'

During the day Reg had learnt that Mr Gray was not only a

farmer but owned a flour mill so he said, 'Yes, I think we would, but I will have to ask David and his father first.'

'All right, I will speak to Lord Sells and he will tell you the decision.'

'Thank you very much, Sir.'

Some twelve brace had been shot in the afternoon. Reg understood that the ground covered was not the best area and that there should be more birds tomorrow. As they walked back to the Lodge Reg told David about the invitation from Mr Gray.

'I don't know Mr Gray and I have never been to his house. Everybody says he is a most extraordinary man who is always experimenting with things. I think it might be quite fun to go, I will see what my father says.'

By the time they had walked back to the Lodge and on to where they were staying they were quite tired. The Earl had given David a brace of grouse to take back to Mrs Williams and he was more than delighted to hand them over.

'Thank you, thank you, Mr David, will you thank His Lordship for me in the morning. I will thank him myself in due time. Now you will be looking for a good tea, I am sure. By the time you have taken off your shoes and had a wash I will be ready.'

Mrs Williams produced a more than adequate meal: soup followed by roast mutton, steam pudding and raspberries and cream. There was not much time for conversation during the meal but once the table was cleared Ted started questioning the boys. Was the shooting good, were there plenty of birds and finally, who were the guns? The boys could not remember the names of them all but they told him of their invitation from Mr Gray.

Ted smiled and said, 'They say that Mr Gray is a very clever man; he is always inventing or trying out new things. To add to that they say that he has three beautiful young daughters,' and he winked at the boys. 'I believe he has just installed a steam engine to drive the mill in place of the water wheel.'

The evening passed quickly with the exchange of family histories. Reg explained that he had a brother who was a soldier and a sister who had just come home from Paris and was at present in London doing the season.

As they walked up to the Lodge next morning they agreed that it would be fun to go and see the flour mill. They soon discovered that Mr Gray and another gun had been replaced by two strangers. They were walking up to the moor when Reg heard his name called.

'Reg, you come and accompany me today.'

'Thank you, Sir.'

He found the Earl just as easy to talk to as his son. He had to explain all about his family, his brother in the army, his sister coming out and all about the estate.

Suddenly the Earl said, 'David says you are very clever.'

'Not really, Sir, but I don't usually find the exams too bad.'

'I have been telling David that he will have to start thinking of something other than horses and cricket.'

Reg, being a bright boy and a good conversationalist, learnt a lot that day. As they were walking back to the lodge Reg thanked the Earl for inviting him for the two days and said how much he had learnt and he continued, 'I forgot to express Mrs Williams' thanks for the grouse. She will thank you personally later, I expect, when she gets rid of us.'

'Thank you, Reg, she is a splendid woman and we are lucky in having them as tenants.'

Reg and David were given strict instructions about the arrangements for the return journey the next day. Once back at the farm they spent another very happy evening. Reg woke early next morning and made a few notes in his journal which he planned to write up when they arrived back at the Lodge.

When the carriage arrived next morning Jack came in to thank Mrs Williams. The boys joined in the thanks. Mrs Williams said she had enjoyed having the young gentlemen and she would be pleased to have them at any time.

The journey home was uneventful but on arrival Jack found a letter from Mr Gray inviting the boys for three nights the following week. He explained that he would be passing by on Tuesday and could pick them up and that he would send them back on Friday. When the proposition was put to them the boys both agreed that they would like to go, so a message to that effect was sent to Mr Gray. During the next few days the boys amused themselves as boys do and Reg found time to write up his journal.

On Tuesday morning about eleven o'clock Mr Gray arrived driving his phaeton which was being drawn by a very well bred looking big dark bay gelding. The boys were ready so after a brief farewell they climbed aboard. They set off at a brisk pace. Mr Gray obviously enjoyed driving fast. They drew up at the same hotel as on the previous week. Mr Gray arranged with the hostler to feed and water his horse before taking the boys in for lunch.

The route from here was different to that to the moors. They followed up a beautiful valley in the centre of which there ran a small river. The gelding, knowing that he was on his way home, trotted out to good purpose and after about two and a half hours they turned into the gates of a private residence. The drive was not long and soon they came in sight of a beautiful country house. It was not large compared to those in which they had been living but it was clearly a very commodious dwelling. They drove straight round to the back where the coachman welcomed his master back.

The boys were both introduced to Bob before picking up their bags and following him into the house.

The girls had heard their father return and were in the hall to greet him and to meet the two boys whom they had heard he was bringing back. May was the same age as David, Caroline just younger than Reg and June two years younger still. Mrs Gray, who had come gliding into the hall, was a big woman of somewhat austere appearance. Why do so many small men marry big women? Mr Gray, having given a quick kiss to his wife and daughters, introduced the boys. The females were all curious to meet David; they had never had a member of a noble family staying in the house before.

After these formalities Mrs Gray asked May to show the boys to their room which, of course, she was delighted to do. She left them saying afternoon tea would be ready in about five minutes and she explained where to find it. The boys soon discovered that Mr Gray's christian name was Rex and his wife's was Pam. The girls called their father, Dad but their mother, Mother. The boys called them Mr and Mrs Gray.

When the table maid had cleared the tea Mr Gray held centre stage and kept the conversation going by asking questions and telling stories. It wasn't long before the atmosphere became very relaxed. At the appropriate moment Mrs Gray announced that it was time for June to go to bed and for everyone else to get ready for dinner. The boys found that their bags had been unpacked and clothes laid out. Dinner turned out to be a very happy family party after which the evening was spent playing card games, many of which the boys had never met before.

After breakfast next morning Mr Gray called to May and said, 'Now, May, you will have to look after the boys this morning, I have other things to do. I suggest that you take them to the farm where the mill is coming in to thrash out those last three stacks, then you can amuse yourselves till lunch time.'

'Yes, Dad,' was all she said as if she did this sort of thing every day.

The boys had never been left in charge of a girl before and did not know what to expect. They soon found out for May, who was rapidly growing into a very pretty girl, was full of confidence, full of knowledge and full of fun. Mr Gray, having no son and a wife who took little interest in things other than those in the house had always taken his eldest daughter about with him. Being a bright girl she had listened to her father's discussions with his staff and so knew most of what was going on. Today it was quite usual for her father to discuss his problems with her.

'Come on, David; come on, Reg, we go this way,' she called as she shot out of the door. As they walked up the road to the farm she asked them if they had ever been to the thrashing.

'No,' replied David.

'I have seen them doing it but don't know anything about it,' was Reg's reply.

As they walked on she explained that the mills were towed from farm to farm by a steam engine which was then used to drive the mill. When it arrived the mill was positioned alongside the stacks; the engine was then unhitched and turned round to face the mill. A driving belt was fitted from the engine to the mill and both vehicles' wheels blocked to ensure they did not move.

They had just reached this stage when they arrived and everyone was having a cup of tea before the hard work began.

The farm manager greeted them with, 'Good morning, Miss May, coming to give us a hand?'

'Good morning, Fred, good morning, everybody. No, we have

just come to see what goes on.'

At that the manager said, 'Come on, lads, we had better get started,' and everybody moved off to their allotted tasks. The engine driver climbed onto his engine, the feed man onto the top of the mill, another climbed up a ladder onto the top of the stack with his fork, while yet another started fitting sacks onto spouts on the side of the mill.

The engine driver, when he saw everybody was in position, gave a short blast on his steam whistle and started up his engine. Everything immediately sprang to life; the man on the stack started throwing sheaves down to the loader who in his turn fed them into the mill. The mill shook while it gobbled up the sheaves. Before long, straw was coming out at the back and grain was flowing into the first sack. As soon as the first bag was full the flow was diverted to the second one and the first one removed and its neck securely tied. David thought it looked a huge sack for one man to lift. It did in fact weigh one cwt. (112 lbs) but the strong man picked it up without difficulty and placed it on an empty four-wheeled waggon which had been put there to receive them. These sacks were destined for the flour mill. The boys kept firing questions at May, all of which she answered.

After about an hour May thought it was time to move on. She showed them round the farm buildings. There was no stock inside apart from a few pigs. That done she walked them down to the village past the flour mill.

'Dad will show you that either this afternoon or tomorrow.'

The mill was situated very close to the railway station and as they went round the back they found a shunting engine pushing two empty waggons up the private siding to the mill. They walked on and arrived back at the house in good time for lunch.

At lunch Mr Gray asked the boys if they had enjoyed the morning.

'Yes,' replied David, 'and May was wonderful, she knew everything.'

'She is a good little farmer is my daughter, she will make a good wife for someone one of these days.' This caused May to blush.

As they were getting up from lunch Mr Gray announced that he would be visiting some farmers in the afternoon and he asked the boys if they would care to accompany him.

'Yes,' they replied and David turned to May and asked her if she would come too.

'Yes, you see I often go with Dad on these visits.'

Dad left the room and May explained to the boys that her father ran a sort of small farm supply and buying and selling agency which many of the smaller farmers took advantage of.

It had turned into a really hot afternoon and May was dressed only in a short sleeved cotton frock and the boys were in their shirt sleeves.

'Come on, then,' said May, 'I expect Dad is out the back waiting for us.'

They found her father already sitting in a two wheeled gig in which there were two seats facing forward and two facing backwards. David surprised himself when he heard himself say, 'Reg, you go in the front and May and I will go in the back.'

They set off and the big gelding was enjoying himself; he even broke into a canter on a few occasions. Suddenly a pheasant flew up from the hedge which caused the gelding to swerve, almost forcing the gig onto one wheel. The two in the back were totally unprepared for this and May was thrown up against David whose arm she clutched. He instinctively held onto her and at that moment he experienced a thrill which he had not felt before.

'Sorry,' she said, pushing herself back into her seat, 'I don't know what took the old boy, but Dad will drive so fast. I tell him he ought to have been named Jehu. Sometimes he lets me drive, but he always says I drive faster than he does.'

'What about asking him if you can drive today and I will come and sit in the front.'

'I doubt if he would let me drive unless he was sitting beside me.'

It was not long before they drew up at a farmhouse. Mr Gray dismounted, saying, 'I won't be long,' and he went straight inside. The three sat down on a wooden bench and enjoyed the sunshine. Reg was able to inform them that it had been a pheasant rising from the hedge which had caused the sudden swerve.

When Mr Gray came out, May said, 'Dad, can I drive?'

'Yes, if you wish to.'

'Can David sit beside me?'

'What if the old boy takes charge?'

'He never has.'

'All right, I want to go and see Mr Wheeler next; come on, Reg, we will climb up behind.'

Once May got the reins in her hand she became like one inspired. She and the old boy appeared to be in complete harmony. They sped on at a great pace, certainly no slower than her father. They cut the corners close but never caught the wheel till finally they drew up at Mr Wheeler's. Mr Gray had never sat in the back while his daughter was driving. He was both thrilled and a little frightened. They had to wait a little longer before he came out this time; as he did so he said, 'Take us to the Ranks' this time.'

They all climbed up into the same seats and off they went. This leg proved to be quite a short one and before long Mr Gray was entering another back door. He came out almost immediately saying that Mr Rank was out but would be back soon. Mrs Rank had invited them all in for a cup of tea. 'May, give the old boy a drink and his tea.'

May led the horse up the yard to the water trough and after he had his drink she removed the bit and fitted the nose bag which they always carried for just such an occasion. They just had time for their cup of tea before Mr Rank returned.

'You run out and get the old boy ready; I shall not be long.'

May, soon had the nose bag off and the bit back in and they were ready for the road again.

'Do you want to take the reins again?'

'Yes, please.'

'All right, but I think I will sit beside you this time.'

If anything she drove faster than ever with the old boy heading for home. By the time they got home the boys were quite glad to get back on firm ground although they had enjoyed the thrill of it.

It was time to change for dinner. Once in their room the boys could not stop talking about May. She was not like any girl they had ever met: she was not only attractive and full of fun, she was so capable at so many things girls did not usually do. During the evening David and May were obviously getting on well together. Reg began to feel a little out of it. He found Caroline such a quiet girl with whom he could not find a common interest. Next morning as they prepared to accompany Mr Gray to the flour mill David asked May, 'Are you coming too?'

'No, I have to do things with Mother this morning, but I will come with you this afternoon.'

As they walked down to the mill, Mr Gray explained that demands for his products had reached the point where the old water wheel could not supply sufficient power so about six months ago he had installed a steam engine. Now they had more than enough power available at all times. He was very proud of his new engine which he showed to them himself before handing them over to Mr Hunter the mill manager. Mr Hunter showed them the grain being fed into the hoppers above the mill stones and how it flowed through the mills into the rotary sheaves and finally into the bags. They saw a stone mason cutting the grooves in the big mill stones. All this took a long time as they had so many questions to ask. It was time for the mill lunch break by the time Mr Hunter delivered them back to Mr Gray's little office. As they walked back Mr Gray said he would be making some more calls that afternoon and asked if they would like to come.

'Oh, yes,' was the reply.

After lunch the four of them, they had been joined by May, went out to find the gig.

'Reg,' Mr Gray called, 'you come up with me this afternoon; the other two can get up behind.' Mr Gray left the driver's seat vacant.

'Shall I sit here?' asked Reg.

'Yes, you can drive this afternoon; I am sure you know what to do.'

He then proceeded to give him a few instructions finishing with, 'Now off you go.'

All went well and Reg found the old boy quite easy to manage. It was another warm day and Mr Gray felt very relaxed and was enjoying being driven by this young man who was doing so well. The old boy was trotting out briskly when on rounding a corner they came face to face with the steam engine towing the mill. This caught everybody off guard. The old boy swerved to the left and broke into a gallop. They were bumping along the grass verge when the near wheel struck one of those little ditches which roadmen dig to carry the water off the road. The gig bounced violently and Mr Gray lost his hold and fell out. Reg, who was struggling to regain control, was hardly aware of what had happened. He himself was having quite a fight to maintain his seat. They had probably only covered some thirty or forty yards before Reg got the old boy back on the road but he had really got the bit between his teeth and was not for stopping. As they rounded a curve, there, not too far away, was a farm cart going in the same direction as themselves. 'What shall I do now, I will never get past that,' but fortunately when the old boy saw it he slackened his pace and Reg was able to regain control. They finally came to a standstill right behind the cart.

After a few seconds to recover his breath he turned round hoping that at least David and May were still there. As he did so he heard May's voice say, 'Well done, Reg, I think I would have panicked.'

'Where is your father, is he hurt?'

'I think he is all right; I saw him get up and walk over to speak to the engine driver. Turn round and go back.'

By this time the old boy had recovered his composure and he trotted back without fuss. Once round the bend they saw in the distance Mr Gray walking towards them limping slightly. When he saw them he waited for them to return. Reg heard May asking her father if he was all right as he himself blurted out, 'I am sorry, Sir, are you hurt, Sir? I didn't know the engine was there and on he went!'

'It wasn't your fault, Reg, I should have been paying more attention and not fallen out like a sack of corn.'

That made Reg feel much better. Mr Gray climbed up with a little difficulty beside Reg saying, 'Come on, we will go on and see old Pettigrew.'

'Are you going to drive, Sir?'

'No, no, you must not allow a little experience like that worry you, you carry on.'

The rest of the afternoon went without a hitch but it was obvious by the time they got home that Mr Gray was getting very stiff. As they climbed down from the gig they noticed a phaeton sitting in the yard, then one of Lord Sells' men appeared with Mr Gray's man. Lord Sells had sent his man up to collect the boys on the following morning. This came as a great relief to Mr Gray as he did not think he would feel like a long drive next day.

Once back in the house May could not resist telling her mother all about the excitements of the afternoon. Mrs Gray, when she heard that her husband had fallen out, began fussing about him, but Mr Gray, having helped himself to a stiff whiskey, went off to have a hot bath after which he felt much better. That evening, like the previous one, was spent playing games. Next morning the boys, having had their breakfast, found their bags packed and ready for them in the hall. It was now time for them to take their leave. The whole family came to see them off. The boys shook hands with the girls and as they did so David said to May, 'You will have to come and stay with us some time.'

'Yes, I would love to do that but you will have to ask my mother.'

'That I will willingly do,' replied David.

They thanked Mr and Mrs Gray saying how much they had enjoyed themselves. They expressed the hope that Mr Gray's stiffness would soon be better. As they were driven home they had plenty of time to discuss all the happenings during their short visit. Mrs Gray, knowing that they would not have time to reach the hotel by lunch time, provided each of them including the coachman with a picnic lunch. At the appropriate time the coachman drew up at a roadside water trough. While he watered and fed his horse the boys sat down at the roadside to eat their lunch. The coachman sat down a respectable distance away.

'Come and sit here,' David called to him so he joined them. The boys told him what a wonderful time they had had and what a capable girl May was. The coachman, in his turn, filled in many details which he had learnt during his stay.

The return journey took longer than the outward one with Mr Gray driving. When they arrived back David's parents had gone to change for dinner, so the boys did likewise. Dinner that night took a long time, the boys had so much to tell. David kept extolling the virtues of May, how she could drive and seemed to know all about the farm.

'Can we have her to stay sometime, you would like her, Mum.'

'I will write to Mrs Gray and make that suggestion.'

Reg's description of his exploits on the box amused Jack very much, especially as Mr Gray was not hurt. 'Mr Gray is a very sporting man, he could very easily have been very angry.'

'He certainly is,' replied Reg, 'I liked him; he was always full of go.'

Reg spent most of the next day writing up his journal and after the weekend's usual Church parade it was time for him to return home.

Chapter 2

Two days before he was due to leave the Lodge, Reg received a letter from his mother instructing him to take the train to London where she would meet him. If she was not at the station he was to take a cab, and she gave an address.

'I shall have to take you to the tailor to be measured for your public school clothes.'

He quite enjoyed the train journey, looking out of the window and day-dreaming about all his experiences while staying with David. He was met at the station by both his mother and Olga. It was too late to go shopping that day so they went straight home. Many people had left London but there were still a few young men whose company Olga enjoyed. That evening another girl and two young men came to dinner after which they played cards while Reg spent the evening recounting all his exploits to his mother. Next morning at breakfast, Mother announced that after shopping she was taking Reg to the Plumbs for lunch. The shopping went well and when lunchtime came, Reg enjoyed meeting Peter and his sisters again. During lunch Aunt May asked Reg if he would like to go to the Zoo that afternoon.

'Oh, yes!'

'Well, Peter and Norah can come but I can't cope with more.'

The children thoroughly enjoyed the Zoo. Surprisingly, Peter and Norah had never been before. They had tea at a restaurant and afterwards as they ate Reg rattled on about the wonderful time he had had with David. When he came to the visit to the Grays he emphasised to Norah what a competent girl May was, how she could drive and knew all about the farm.

'Oh! I would love to be able to do that,' exploded Norah.

'Well,' replied Reg, 'you and Peter will have to come and stay and have a go with us.'

The Plumbs dropped Reg off on their way home where he learnt that he was to accompany Olga and his mother to the theatre that evening. The play was a light-hearted comedy at which he laughed a lot.

Next morning all three were to return home. Reg was amazed at the amount of luggage the ladies had accumulated while in London; it required a cab and a dray to convey it to the station. The party, of course, included the ladies' maid but the other London servants had been hired for the season.

Reg thought that once back home life would be dull but it did not prove to be so. He had much to talk to his father about and he persuaded him to allow him to practise driving with the coachmen any time they were going on an errand. Otherwise he divided his time between visits to Tom, and working in the garden and on the farm where he was determined to learn what was going on. And so the holidays slipped away and it was time for him to go to his public school.

He took the train to London where he reported to David's grandfather's town house. He was delighted to find Lord and Lady Sells there as well as David. That evening the four of them dined in quite a small but very smart restaurant, before going on to see a play. The theatre was quite small and the play turned out to be a thriller. The acting was so good that Reg really felt he was part of the plot. Next day Jack took the two boys down and handed them over to their new housemaster. Everything was very different to their prep. school but being together it was much less alarming. It was not long before they got into the new routines and the mysteries of fagging, etc.

The abilities of the two boys being so different, they inevitably began to make friends with different boys. Reg, who was now so much more self-confident, enjoyed school; he especially enjoyed battles of wits. Because of their age difference they had been placed in different forms but he and David often met and compared notes.

His first letter came from Mary and was the start of a regular correspondence between them. Mary kept him prompted with all the gossip while he felt he could write her about goings-on at school about which he would never write to his parents. Mary passed on what she thought was appropriate to them. Great was his surprise when he received a letter from his father. It was not a very long letter but gave him some information about happenings at home and enquired how he was getting on. He wrote quite a long reply. Reg was in fact a good letter writer.

On returning home for the Christmas holidays he received a great welcome from Mary. She was finding life very dull at home; although Olga was living at home she went away a lot and at other times spent most of her time with her mother. One day when Reg was pottering about the farm talking to the workers he ran in to Mr Oliver, the young agent who had recently taken over from his father.

'Hello, Master Reg, are you trying to find out what goes on up here?'

This was the start of quite a long conversation in which Reg told Ken all about his visit to David and especially about the few days with the Grays. Reg finished by saying, 'I would like to know all about the farm like May does.'

'Very good; we could start next Tuesday if you could be here at nine thirty. Will you talk to your father and obtain his agreement?'

'Yes, thank you, see you next Tuesday.'

Great was Reg's surprise when he received a letter from Penny from Australia wishing him a Happy Christmas. Although she was so much older than him she had made Christmas such fun for him last year, he wished she was here this year.

His father was delighted that he was taking so much interest in the farm and arranged for him to come and tell him what he had discovered each time he met Ken Oliver.

Christmas came and went, Arthur brought young men to shoot and Olga had some of her friends to stay and there were parties. Somehow, neither he nor Mary fitted in, but Mary was becoming more and more a young lady and less inclined to join in his pursuits. He only managed two visits to the farm with Ken before it was time to return to school. The Easter term was largely a matter of routine. He played games when he had to, holding his own but without distinction. In the classroom things were better; here he excelled and was the brightest boy of his age group. His father was delighted with his school report as he had never anticipated having a scholar in the family.

Once home, Reg sent a note to Ken asking when they could meet. He received a reply suggesting a date and inviting him to return for lunch with him. Reg readily accepted the invitation and after an interesting morning on the farm they returned to the Willows for lunch. Ken had grown up at the Willows but on leaving school had left home to learn his trade. The Willows was a small farm on the property, the tenancy of which went with the job of agent. Reg did not know what family Ken had but he knew he was married. It did not take them long to cover the two and a half miles in the pony trap which Ken used to go round the farms. As they stepped from the trap a very smiling young lady came through the door.

'This is my wife Olive.'

Reg wondered if he had heard correctly. Surely it could not be Olive Oliver? He was reassured as she said, 'I know you don't believe it but it is true, I am Olive Oliver. Come away in; I have heard a lot about you.'

Once inside Olive called out, 'Come along, girls, come and meet Master Reg.'

There was a clatter of feet and in ran two girls just about Reg's age. Reg could not believe his eyes: they were identical. He had never met twins before. Although he had thought he was overcoming his shyness with girls he was quite taken aback.

'This is Ann and this is Isobel.'

'How-do-you-do, I am afraid I shall never know you apart.'

'Never mind, nobody ever does.'

They sat down to lunch with the two girls sitting together opposite Reg. There was a silence for a moment which was broken by Olive saying, 'We have heard so much about your trip north; do tell us all about it.'

This was enough to set the girls off and their questions came thick and fast. They had learnt quite a bit from their father. Reg tried to answer their questions but after a while he began to realise that he was having his leg pulled by them. He counter-attacked by giving some obviously impossible answers. In no time they might have known one another for years.

Ken did not wish to interrupt the young people but eventually he said, 'I am sorry, Reg, but I shall have to take you home. I am going to see Mr Wood this afternoon; would you like to see his farm on the way home?'

Mr Wood's farm was not very different to the home farm but he had a larger dairy. Reg enjoyed meeting Mr Wood and seeing his farm.

That evening at dinner Reg recounted his surprise when he discovered at lunch that the Olivers had twin daughters. He emphasized what nice girls they were. His father turned to his wife and said, 'You have never met young Ken and I have never met his wife and daughters. I think we should ask them down for tea while Reg is at home,' so that was arranged for the following week. The tea party went well and both Olga and Mary were fascinated to meet the twins. None of them could tell them apart.

It was during this holiday that Arthur came home on leave. He was full of the idea that they should build a lawn tennis court. Several chaps in his regiment had started to play and he had got quite keen. He obtained his father's agreement and a site was selected. Arthur then engaged a contractor to supervise the work, with the estate providing most of the labour. This work had just begun when it was time for Reg to return to school.

He enjoyed the summer term: cricket was fun although he was not much good at it, unlike David. He also learnt to swim and by the end of term could do several lengths of the bath. This holidays he was invited once again to join the Plumbs at the seaside. He expected this would be even more fun now that he could swim. When the end of term came he returned home before joining the Plumbs. He found the tennis court finished but the grass was not sufficiently thick for it to be played on yet. They hoped it would be by the time he came home from the seaside. He was now quite used to travelling by himself by train and Peter met him at the station.

Having collected his luggage, Peter said, 'You tell the porter to send your bags to the hotel and you come with me.'

Once this was done they left the station and there leaning against the wall was a bicycle, one of the new safety bicycles; it even had pneumatic tyres. Peter's father had bought it and Peter had just learnt to ride it. They proceeded to a grassy area where Reg had his first lesson. This machine provided hours of entertainment for the two boys. The holiday went well with fishing, swimming and the bicycle, but there was no longer any idea of dashing into the girls' room: they were getting too grown up for that.

On returning home, Reg found that the tennis court was now deemed ready to be played on and Arthur was coming next week to take it over from the makers. A rustic tennis shelter had been built with an area at the back to house the mower, nets and line marker. Also provided were four gentlemen's rackets and two ladies' ones and, of course, a box of twelve tennis balls.

When Arthur returned he brought with him a friend with whom he was to demonstrate his prowess as a tennis player. Having satisfied himself that everything was in order, the two young men got dressed up in their long white tennis flannels and started hitting balls back and forward across the net. Reg watched with interest and when they started playing a game he tried to understand the rules and the scoring. During the next few days he, Olga and Mary were all given lessons in the art of tennis playing. Reg made reasonable progress but the girls were hopeless.

He restarted his farm visits with Ken and was once more invited back for lunch. He enjoyed meeting the twins again. He discovered that Olive and the twins were familiar with most of the games he had learnt with the Grays. He became quite a regular visitor at the Olivers' table.

Of his sisters, Mary showed the greatest potential as a tennis player so from time to time he persuaded her to practise with him. They both made reasonable progress but he could always beat his sister. And so, between the garden, the tennis court, the farm and the Olivers the holidays slipped away. At his request the twins agreed to write to him when he returned to school telling him what was going on on the farm. Before returning to school he asked his father if he would buy him a bicycle. This request was not too well received, with his father saying, 'I cannot see what you want one of those things for.'

Back at school he found himself in a higher form and once again the youngest boy.

After a week he received his first letter from the twins; it was signed by Ann. The next week he received one signed by Isobel. Their writing was so alike he could not tell the difference. Ken encouraged these letters as it stimulated an interest in the farm by the girls. School life being so routine Reg found it difficult to find subject matter for his letters so he started telling them something about what he was learning, particularly history which he thought would interest them. As time went on little messages such as 'we miss you' began to creep into the girls' letters, then the odd cross at the bottom. Olive longed to know what was in this correspondence but never enquired.

Back home again for the Christmas holidays he began his chess games with his father. It was on such an occasion that he asked his father some questions about the farm.

'How did you hear about that?' replied his father, 'that happened while you were at school.'

'I don't know, I just heard.' He did not disclose his correspondence with the twins.

He started to learn to shoot with John. He proved to be a natural and made rapid progress, but in spite of that he was not all that enthusiastic about killing things.

One day when he was visiting the Olivers he was sitting on a stool looking at a book when one of the twins came up behind him, put her arms round him and kissing him said, 'Guess who that was?' He was taken quite by surprise as he had never had any physical contact like that before. He was beginning to develop and his attitude towards girls was just beginning to change. He thought for a second and then said, 'I don't know, do it again, you took me by surprise last time.' This time it was of course the other twin. From that moment on the relationship between them began to change ever so slightly and he enjoyed it.

There was the usual shoot and dance at New Year. He stayed up for dinner but did not participate in the dance.

The Easter term came and went during which he really enjoyed his correspondence with the twins. The subject matter expanded and they had some quite long and challenging debates.

Lack of time almost became a problem during the Easter holidays. He enjoyed the breeding of the pheasants more than shooting them; he continued to ride and drive the carriage on occasion. Then there was the garden, the farm and visits to the Willows. One day when he was at the farm Ken turned to him and said, 'Just a minute, I must just go and see if the young bull is working all right.'

'Can I come too?'

'Yes,' and so he witnessed for the first time this act which turned out to be a much shorter and simpler matter than he expected. However, this did lead to a long discussion on animal reproduction. He had picked up some ideas on the subject before but now he had a very clear and matter of fact explanation of the subject. That afternoon when he was out for a walk with the twins Ann said, 'Well, what did you and Dad do on the farm this morning?'

He did not know exactly how to answer. He felt embarrassed as he knew that this was a subject which you did not discuss with girls, but did not know why.

'Oh, well, just how long it took cows to have calves and that sort of thing.'

'What do you mean?' asked Isobel.

'I think you had better ask your mother; she will explain it much better than I could.'

There the subject was left. That evening when the girls were going to bed Isobel said to her mother, 'Reg told us this afternoon that Dad had been telling him all about how long it took for a cow to have a calf and things like that. He said he could not explain it but to ask you.'

'Oh, dear; I knew this moment must come. I tell you what I will do. We will start a biology class and I will tell you a little bit each evening.'

After the girls had gone to bed Olive asked Ken what he had been doing with Reg that day which had caused such interest. The girls found their evening sessions with their mother most fascinating and as the mysteries of reproduction unfolded they began to feel very grown up.

Back at school Reg once again enjoyed the summer term especially as he knew that at the end of it he would be sufficiently senior to be free from fagging and other such undignified duties.

The plan for this summer holidays was for Reg and his cousin Peter to go together to stay with their Aunt Edith who lived in St Andrews in Fife, Scotland. Aunt Edith was married to Professor Robert McKenzie who taught at the University. Both boys had heard of Uncle Robert and Aunt Edith but had never met them and in fact knew very little about them.

Reg went to London and spent the night with Peter and next

morning they caught the train from Kings Cross. It was a through train for Aberdeen but they had to leave it at Leuchars and take the local train to St Andrews. The journey was a long one but as there were two of them the time passed quite quickly. They were met at the station by Uncle Robert and his son Ben. Ben was a year older than the boys and both he and his father were very tall. Uncle Robert looked much too young to be a professor. He arranged for the luggage to be delivered and they set off to walk home. They did not have far to walk and on arrival got a great welcome from Aunt Edith, Mary who was a year younger than them and John who was younger still. The two boys shared a room in what was quite a large house.

Robert McKenzie, a son of the manse, had been born in Sutherland. After school in the north he went to Edinburgh University from where he emerged with an honours degree in agriculture and horticulture. From there he became a research worker at Cambridge University. It was while working there that he took a six week holiday job to tutor a boy for his University exam and while staying in this large country house he had first met Edith. Their romance developed slowly and it was two years before they were married. By this time he had acquired his PhD. There followed a four-year appointment at McGill University in Canada before he returned to Cambridge as a lecturer. His two hobbies were the countryside and golf. It was the latter which prompted his application and appointment to his present chair. Although he had only been in St Andrews less than three years he had already been elected a member of the Royal and Ancient Golf Club.

Robert was a tremendous enthusiast and his son had inherited this trait. They were a difficult pair to keep up with. That first evening was spent exchanging information, but next morning the two boys were taken straight down to the local golf pro and handed over to him for tuition. After spending the whole morning hitting golf balls on a piece of waste ground they were deemed to have acquired sufficient skill to be allowed onto the golf course. Uncle Robert and Ben were so much better than them but Uncle Robert produced a wonderful system of handicaps which somehow always kept them in the game. They played golf mostly in St Andrews but they visited Crail, Elie and Lundin Links, all of which were within easy reach of the railway. They explored the town but it was the expeditions into the country which Reg enjoyed most. On these occasions the whole family were present. They nearly always carried their lunch. Sometimes they walked from the town, sometimes they took the train for one or two stations and then walked. Without Uncle Robert these trips would have been dull, but he never allowed their interest to lag; he was always telling them about things which they never even knew existed, from birds to bugs, from rocks to soil, from seeds to trees, there did not seem to be anything he did not know about the countryside. Reg, with his interest in farming and gardening, lapped up all this information, but a lot of it went over Peter's head.

On Sunday they all went to the Parish Church. It was a beautiful large building but the service was quite different to the one they were accustomed to. Uncle Robert explained that he had been brought up as a Presbyterian, and there followed a long explanation all about the Reformation. Reg had never paid much attention to what he had been taught about this subject but once again Uncle Robert made it so interesting he decided that he should change his ways.

That night Reg entered in his journal, 'I must tell you about some of our expeditions into the country; there is one I especially remember, it was near the end of our stay. We had already walked round the coast at the golf course. On one side is the open sea and on the other an estuary. This day we were to go to the other side of the estuary. We took the train to Leuchars and then walked from there. It was not far to the estuary and we walked towards its mouth. The tide was out and there were miles of mud flats. We saw so many different kinds of waders I can't remember them all. Then we saw seals not far out on the mud. When we got to the end we turned left along the shore. The sea seemed to be miles away beyond an immense expanse of flat sand and the sun was getting very hot. Uncle Robert suggested we leave the beach and follow along amongst the sand dunes and scrub where there were so many more things of interest. Ben kept searching for a rare plant which his father said could sometimes be found in that area. We kept on putting up rabbits, including many young ones. I tried to catch one of the little ones but they were always too quick for me. After some considerable time spent this way we rounded a sand dune and there was the sea almost covering the immense expanse of sand.

'"What about a dip before lunch," suggested Aunt Edith, "the water should be very warm after coming in over all that hot sand."

'"Good idea," we all replied. Whenever we went on a walk near the sea we always took our swimming things with us. The water was indeed warm and we had to wade miles out to find water deep enough to swim in. After some half an hour or so it was deemed time to return for lunch. We hung our swim suits and towels out on the bushes to dry during lunch. As we munched our sandwich Uncle Robert said to me, "Reg have you thought what you will do when you leave school; will you follow your brother into the army?"

'"I don't want to go into the army, I think I would like to go to Cambridge and study agriculture.'

'"Well, if in a year or two's time you still wish to do that, let me know and I am sure I could be of some help to you.'

'"Thank you very much."

'After lunch it was time for us to start to make our way back to the station. After a short time we picked up a track which appeared to be heading in the right direction. On rounding a bend we came face to face with a man who was obviously a gamekeeper; he was carrying a gun and had two spaniels at his feet.

'"Good afternoon Professor, you have a big party with you today."

'They obviously knew one another well.

'"Yes," replied my Uncle, "we have been down for a swim. What are you after?"

'"As a matter of fact I am looking for a fox earth. I have been losing birds and there is no sign of the old boy at any of the usual earths; I think they must have opened a new one somewhere."

'"Good luck in your search, nice to see you John."

'" Thank you, Sir," and touching his cap he continued on his way.

'Uncle Robert explained, "John is a great character, he knows this area like the back of his hand. He has helped me to find some interesting specimens." The walk back to the station on such a hot day seemed a long one and we were quite glad to sit down on the old wooden seat at the station and wait for the train.'

The boys met several of Ben's friends either on the golf course or on the beach which in turn led to invitations out for meals. This sort of social life was new to Reg but familiar to Peter.

Reg tried hard to keep his journal up to date and in particular to record the names and addresses of the many people he met.

All too soon the holiday was over and Ben accompanied them to Leuchars and saw them on to the London train. The train was fairly full but they found two seats in a compartment whose only occupants were a young couple, much Arthur and Olga's age. They were of course travelling first class, as was usual for persons in their social group. The young couple were occupying the window seats so the boys settled down to read the books they had brought for the journey. After a short time the young man, who did not seem to have anything to occupy him, turned to Reg and enquired where they were travelling to.

'We are going to London, are you going to London too?'

'No, we are getting off in York, we live in Yorkshire. Do you live in London?'

'He does,' and Reg pointed at Peter, 'but I live some fifty miles north west of London in the country. We are cousins.'

The ice was broken and from then on conversation never lagged. The young couple had only been married six months and Jane had come from London, so there was plenty of common ground. Max and Jane invited the boys to join them for lunch after leaving Edinburgh and so York was reached without a dull moment. Reg's previous holiday in Yorkshire with David produced much for him and Max to talk about. He knew Lord and Lady Sells slightly but had never met his father. He was much amused by the story of Mr Gray falling out when he was driving. He had never heard of Mr Gray. He and his wife were returning from their first fishing trip. He had not ever fished before but had a wonderful gillie to help him. The gillie made casting look so easy he could not understand why he himself found it so difficult. By the end of the week he was getting on quite well.

'Did you catch anything?' asked Reg.

'Yes, it was not a very big one, only eight pounds, but it was exciting.'

A similar situation existed between Jane and Peter. Neither of them knew anything about salmon fishing but they did know about life in London. On arrival at York the two boys moved over into the two window seats in their non-smoking compartment. They were joined by two elderly ladies, well, they looked at least as old as their mothers. Being well mannered boys, they offered the window seats to the ladies. Their offer was suitably declined. Soon after leaving York the lady sitting next Reg turned to him and said, 'It was very good of you to offer us the window seats but we both know the country well. We both live in Yorkshire but our hobby is travelling and we usually start by going to London.'

When the two ladies had entered the compartment the boys' hearts had sunk as they visualised a pretty dull trip. Little did they realise what it would turn out to be.

Reg's neighbour started in right away, 'I am Miss Brough and my friend is Miss Long.'

They both started questioning the boys, where had they been and where did they live? The boys explained that they were cousins and had been staying with their uncle and aunt in St Andrews. They really enjoyed recounting all about their holiday, its golf and the expeditions into the country. Reg went on to describe his previous holiday in Yorkshire with David. This greatly amused the ladies as they seemed to know everyone Reg mentioned. Before long it was time for afternoon tea and they all found their way to the first class dining car. It soon became apparent that Miss Brough was the dominant partner and Reg felt that he was getting on so well with her he could start quizzing her about her travels.

'Where do you usually travel to, Miss Brough?' enquired Reg.

'That is a very good question,' replied Miss Long. 'The problem is to know where to start. As we both knew some French and German we started making summer trips there. We slowly migrated south to Italy and Spain. This meant learning something of those languages as it is no fun if you cannot talk to the locals.'

The journey was passing rapidly and trips to Norway and Sweden were described.

'Where are you going this time? The summer has nearly gone,' asked Reg.

'Well, of recent years we have been going further afield. Two years ago we spent nearly a year in India and this time we are taking a boat to East Africa. We have never explored that continent before. Would you be interested to read of some of our trips?'

'Yes,' replied Reg and he was given a list of books written by them. By this time they were rolling into King's Cross.

'Good-bye, Miss Brough, good-bye Miss Long,' Reg said.

'Good-bye boys, we hope we have not bored you.'

'Certainly not, I am going to buy some of your books,' was Reg's parting shot.

Peter said, as they jogged along in the cab to his home, 'What an extraordinary pair, I never expected that when they came into the compartment.'

That night they were late in getting to bed as they described all the exploits of their holiday, not forgetting the meeting with the Misses Brough and Long. Next morning *en route* for the station Reg stopped at a bookshop and ordered a copy of *India* by Mary Brough and Jane Long.

On arriving home Reg found both Olga and Mary were away staying with friends. That meant long evenings alone with his parents. Being on their own, their conversation tended to take on a more serious nature and they discussed all manner of things. Reg greatly enjoyed these evenings and began to get closer to his mother. She was delighted to hear about her sister Edith. Edith, being considerably the youngest of the family, had always tended to be a bit of a loner and she had felt she was losing touch with her.

Ken Oliver, having discovered that Reg was home again, invited him up to lunch. This was a very popular move as he was beginning to find life rather dull on his own. As soon as he arrived he was struck by how much the twins had grown up. However, they greeted him with great enthusiasm and seemed just the same to talk to. The conversation at lunch flitted back and forth. Ken was most interested to hear about Uncle Robert's amazing knowledge of ornithology and botany, but truth to tell it was the ladies who monopolised the conversation.

'Is it true that Miss Mary is off to Paris soon?' asked Olive.

'I have not seen her but Mother said she was going in September.'

'And what about Miss Olga, a little bird has been whispering about various young men seeking her hand.'

'That's her business, not mine,' replied Reg..

After lunch the three young people went for a walk up the lane. As they walked Isobel took Reg's hand, saying, 'We have missed you, it seems ages since we saw you.'

'We haven't exactly lost touch, I have enjoyed receiving your letters.'

'We have all yours safe in a drawer,' replied Ann.

It was a glorious hot day so they decided to sit down on a bank. The girls placed themselves one on each side of him. Reg thought to himself, if some of my school friends could see me now with a pair of goodlooking twins sitting on either side of me, I wouldn't half get my leg pulled. The afternoon soon slipped away, they had so much to talk about, not least the meeting with Mary Brough and Jane Long.

Ann said, 'Mum has told us all about how animals are

reproduced so you need not be shy about talking about those things just because we are there.'

There followed a long silence then Reg got up and offering a hand to each girl pulled them up and they sauntered home together. Reg invited the girls down to play tennis but even after Mary was home and they were four Reg did not find it much fun. He felt he could not hit the ball hard at the girls. He started spending more and more time at the farm, sometimes with Ken and sometimes just with the men.

Olga came and went; she seemed to have lots of invitations to house parties. Soon it was time for Mary to leave for Paris and for him to return to school. He had almost forgotten about India when his father called him into his study and presented him with a small parcel.

'This is addressed to you, Reg, not me. It looks like a book to me.'

Reg opened it and as he did so the bill fell out onto the floor. Reg explained about his ordering the book on his way home. His father took the book and had a quick look through it then handed it back, saying, 'It looks most interesting; give me the bill, I will see to that.'

'Thank you, Father,' he said.

'You can lend it to me when you have read it,' was his father's reply.

He took the book back to school with him and found it so interesting he read it and re-read it. The two ladies accompanied by a small staff travelled all over India, visiting many places not normally visited by white ladies on their own.

That term, at his father's suggestion, he started attending confirmation classes with a view of being confirmed at school. When the day of confirmation arrived he found himself almost of two minds. On the one hand he wished to commit himself but on the other hand he was not sure that he was really sure what it meant for him. There was, of course, no thought of his not going through with it.

Back at Wantock life was very quiet that Christmas. Arthur was serving overseas and Mary was not coming home. There were only his parents and Olga at home. He began to spend more time with his father, sometimes playing chess, sometimes talking generally, including such things as shooting, hunting and the Estate. He also raised the subject of what he wanted to do on leaving school in a little over a year's time. He said he wished to go to Cambridge and read agriculture and that he was going to write to Uncle Robert and get his advice. This plan was welcomed by his father.

One evening, when they had just finished a game of chess, his father, whose conversation was always brief and to the point, suddenly said to him, 'Reg, I always meant to ask you, how did the confirmation go?' and before he had time to answer his father continued, 'Religion is one of those things which we fathers often find difficult to discuss with our children. I suppose it is because we know so little about it ourselves. It is a wonderful thing and the more you know about it the better; it is a great help as a guide in life.'

Thereupon he got up and crossing the room took a white box from a cupboard. He handed it to Reg, saying, 'I meant to bring this to the confirmation but as you know we could not get there in the end.'

Reg opened the box and inside was a brand new bible.

'Thank you, Sir, I know I shall always treasure it.' At that his father patted him on the shoulder and bade him goodnight.

One new venture which he started this holidays was to attend several meets of the local foxhounds. Mounted on one of his father's hunters and accompanied by a groom, they hacked on to any meet within a radius of about seven miles. He enjoyed watching the hounds working and found the chase a great thrill. His father had more or less given up hunting which made his horses available.

Not surprisingly, he also spent quite a lot of time with the Olivers. He enjoyed the company of the twins; they used to play games as well as indulge in a lot of light-hearted conversation. He knew the girls so well now they were almost like sisters to him.

One day towards the end of the holidays a young man called the Hon. John Goodho arrived to stay the night. Reg had met him before when he had been at one of the parties but there was obviously more to this visit. When they assembled for dinner, champagne was being served. John had obtained his wish, the hand of Olga in marriage, and the engagement was being celebrated.

In the hunting field Reg had met several young people of his own age group. In particular he had become friendly with a trio, a brother and sister and another boy. They were all hacking home one evening with the father of the brother and sister when Reg asked them if they would care to come and dine at Wantock one evening. They all thought that would be fun and their father said they could all go in one carriage which would mean only one man being required. Reg agreed to consult his parents and then send them an invitation. When Reg raised the proposition with his parents they were delighted as he had never shown any social inclinations before. A date was fixed and the Oliver twins were invited to square off the numbers. When the date arrived his parents rose to the occasion and welcomed the guests most warmly. After dinner the young people retired to the library where they played cards and other games. The party went well and there was much laughter.

Reg wrote his letter to Uncle Robert and in reply received an invitation to St Andrews in the Easter holidays when the question of Cambridge could be discussed. And so another holiday had come and gone. Once back at school he continued his correspondence with the Oliver twins. He had lent them the book on India which, as they read it, proved a great subject for their letters.

Being in the same house, Reg maintained his friendship with David. He invited him to join him in his trip to St Andrews in the Easter holidays, subject to his Uncle Robert's approval. Uncle Robert readily agreed and suggested they travel on a day which was some five days after the end of term. This gave both boys time to go home and sort out their clothes, they were getting to the age when this mattered to them. The plan was for Reg to leave the day before and spend the night in London with Peter before catching the train next morning. David was to join the train at York.

When the day came Reg was walking along the platform looking for a seat when he noticed a compartment occupied by two girls of his sort of age. What overtook him he did not know but he opened the door and asked if he might join them. They were thrilled to welcome him.

As he sat down he said, 'I do hope you don't mind my suggesting joining you but on previous long journeys I have been greatly entertained by the company I have met on the journey. May I ask how far you're travelling?

'We are returning from school to Edinburgh where we both live,' they replied.

'I too will be passing through Edinburgh and I am sure your company will greatly shorten the journey.' He introduced himself and asked their names.

'Oh, I am Helen Murray and my father is a lawyer,' 'And I am Catherine Rowe and my father is a doctor.'

The ice was now broken and the conversation flowed freely. The girls were thrilled to have Reg with them, he was such a good conversationalist. David joining them at York was an even greater thrill especially when they learnt of his background. David's more lighthearted conversation came just at the right moment to enliven the rest of the journey.

As they drew into Waverley station Reg was surprised to see Ben on the platform. He was talking to John Murray who had come to meet the girls. When they alighted from the train the boys and the girls had already exchanged addresses, but this meeting with two more boys sparked off more chatter, the outcome of which was a plan for them all to meet on Friday for the Charity Ball. Helen, whose mother was involved in the ball organisation, said she would write to Reg and tell him of the plan they had made.

It was now time for Ben and the other two to continue their journey. Once back in the train Ben said, 'You realise what you have let yourselves in for?'

'What do you mean?' said David.

'First we will have to come back to Edinburgh on Friday morning and we will be billeted on various houses – so far so good – but the dance in the evening will be chiefly Scottish country dances. Do you know them?'

'No,' was the reply.

'That means that Mary and I will be very busy.'

The house in St Andrews was a new experience for David.

Here there were no male staff, in fact there were only a cook, a tablemaid, a housemaid and a between maid. That first evening was spent getting up to date with news and planning the week ahead. It was agreed that first thing next morning Ben would take David and initiate him into the game of golf. Ben was confident he would have David ready to take his place in a family four-ball in the afternoon. Reg was to stay behind and talk to his uncle about Cambridge.

As was expected, David took to golf like a duck to water and that afternoon and on the following day two memorable family games were held. As they had only arrived on Tuesday and were to leave again on the following Monday the dance in Edinburgh caused a great disruption to the expected programme. On Thursday Reg received the expected letter which invited not only the three boys but also Mary to the ball. The letter expressed the hope that they could arrive on the train which reached Edinburgh at 3.00 pm where they would be met. Receipt of this letter caused a degree of consternation, first Mary and her mother had to find the necessary clothes and the boys rather wished that they had not got embroiled as they would have preferred to play golf on Friday and Saturday. However, the die was cast so they were determined to make the best of it. As they were such a male dominated party the McKenzies invited two girls for dinner on the Thursday evening. This proved a bonus for Reg and David as it gave them another opportunity to practise the Scottish dances.

When the St Andrews party arrived in Edinburgh they found John, Helen and Catherine waiting for them. They learnt that Ben and Mary were to be staying with the Murrays and Reg and David with the Rowes. When the cab finally came to a stop at the Rowes' house it proved to be one of the larger town houses. Catherine ran up the steps and pulled the bell. On the door being opened

Mrs Rowe came forward to greet them which was quite unexpected.

'Mother, this is David and this is Reg.'

Having greeted the two boys, Mrs Rowe turned to a young girl who was standing behind her, saying, 'Come on, Rosemary, come and meet the boys.'

These formalities over, they moved into a large drawing-room where afternoon tea was served. Mrs Rowe, who took complete charge of proceedings, quickly made it clear to the boys that her husband was one of the top members of the medical profession in Edinburgh. Having established her position she proceeded to question the boys on their families. When she learnt of David's lineage he quickly took pride of place in her attentions.

After some time Mrs Rowe turned to Catherine and said, 'Go and see if your father is ready for his tea.'

Dr Rowe's consulting room, although within the house, had a separate entrance.

She returned, saying, 'He is just coming.'

Dr Rowe was a shortish man, slightly overweight and with greying hair. He greeted the boys most cordially and the conversation brightened up. It emerged that a dinner party for twelve was to be held in the house, six residents and six from the Murrays. In due time the boys were shown their rooms and told the time of dinner. As this was a Charity Ball and aimed primarily at the younger generation, full ball dress was optional. When they assembled for dinner the boys were in their dinner suits and the girls in long frocks. Mrs Rowe did not wear her jewels, just a long string of pearls. When the Murrays arrived the scene changed. Both Mr Murray and John were dressed in kilts as was Ben whose tartan was of course different. The girls all wore tartan sashes. Dressed for the occasion, Mary stood out, not only was she taller but she had a much better figure, and to crown all she possessed the most beautiful features and disarming smile.

Reg found himself sitting between Helen and Rosemary at dinner. He could not have been better pleased with his companions. Both proved good conversationalists. At the start of the dancing the two English boys felt somewhat nervous but as time passed they warmed to the task and what were impossible moves at the beginning began to come more easily. Both boys did their duty with their hostesses. David, who had already been attracted to Mary, fell for her; not only was she one of the best lookers, she was one of the best dancers. When the dancing finally stopped Reg, who had not been looking forward to the whole affair, discovered that he had really enjoyed himself. The Scottish country dances introduced a wonderful element of gaiety and informality to the proceedings. The following afternoon they returned to St Andrews. The rest of the weekend passed without incident as did the return journey on Monday.

Once home again, Reg discussed with his father his wish to go to Cambridge. The principle was quickly agreed and a decision taken to take the subject up with his school. There were now not many days of his holiday left but Reg found time to meet the Oliver twins and to tell them all about the Scottish country dances. When he told them of his plan to go to Cambridge, Isobel said she wanted to go to London and study medicine. Her sister said she wanted to learn to become a teacher with a view of becoming a governess to a wealthy family who indulged in overseas travel.

'So you two are planning to go your separate ways; how exciting, your letters should become more interesting. It's all a long time ahead. I wonder what we will in fact do when the time comes.'

Once back at school he went to see his housemaster and told

him of him of his desire to go to Cambridge and of his talks with his Uncle Robert. His housemaster was delighted and expressed the view that he should have no trouble passing the exams and added, 'Were you thinking of trying for a scholarship?'

'Yes, I should like to try if you think I would have any chance.'

It was left for further consideration but in the meantime his name would be entered for the college suggested by Uncle Robert. Some time later he was surprised to receive a letter from Olga saying that her wedding had been fixed for the first week of the summer holidays and advising him not to arrange any trips for that week. The date had been chosen because Arthur would be home on leave at that time.

Reg, who had always been slow to make friends, had now established a good circle of them. One day he was sitting watching a cricket match with one of these friends and the conversation came round to the summer holidays. Reg disclosed that his sister was getting married and that that would not only occupy his parents but would be a considerable financial drain. His companion replied that they would be going to Drumliff.

'Where is that?' replied Reg.

'It's in the west highlands of Scotland; my father bought it some years ago. It's great fun, we have fishing, deer stalking and some rough shooting. Would you like to come up?' and he continued, 'The only problem is getting there; it is a two days' journey each way. You have to take the train to Glasgow, the overnight boat to Fort William and the post bus to the lodge.'

They discussed the project for some time and Reg became more and more interested in the idea. It was left that Reg would write to his father and ask his permission and whether he would make the necessary funds available. Reg thought that his father would lend him some fishing tackle. He did not write to his father immediately but with his experience of travelling to Scotland behind him he wrote to the travel agent setting out exactly what he wished to do and asking for a detailed plan with costs. On receipt of this information he wrote to his father, setting out the project in detail and enclosed a copy of the travel agent's report in support of his request for funds. He was well aware that the best way to obtain his father's agreement was to cause him the least possible effort. He wished to have the whole thing agreed before he came home and got involved in the wedding. Reg opened his father's letter with some trepidation but was greatly relieved to receive his father's approval and the information that he knew the Wilsons. Armed with this consent he confirmed with Robin Wilson that he would love to accept his invitation. Robin replied that he would ask his father for a suitable date and if there would be anyone else coming at the same time. If two or more people arrived together his father thought it worth while to send his wagonette to meet them which was not only quicker but much more comfortable than the post bus.

Some time later Robin said that he had heard from his father telling him that his Uncle Sam would be leaving London on the first of September and that he had written to him asking him to contact Reg to arrange the time and place they should meet in London. Some days later Reg received the following letter.

Dear Reg,
I am looking forward to travelling north with you on 1st September next. Please report to the head porter at the station hotel on or before nine o'clock that day. I will arrange for the porter to introduce you to me.
Yours sincerely
Samuel Wilson

The letter was written from a club in London. Reg acknowledged the letter, stating that he would be happy to follow these instructions, and informed his father of his plans.

It was not long before the end of term came and Reg returned home. There he found what to him seemed general confusion. Contractors were erecting a marquee on the lawn and there appeared to be staff everywhere. He was glad to learn that his cousin Peter Plumb would be sharing his room with him. The other piece of good news was that the whole McKenzie family were coming down. The next few days until the guests arrived he kept as far away from the house as possible, visiting the garden, the farm and the Oliver twins. By the afternoon before the wedding the old house was bursting at the seams and all the old nursery wing was fully occupied.

Reg and his two cousins, Ben and Peter, thought that they must do something to ensure the young couple had a good send-off. Reg suggested that they might get the local huntsman to come and blow 'Gone away' on the hunting horn as their carriage drew away.

The great day came and the local church was packed. The reception made a very colourful scene in the marquee. Uncle Robert proposed the main toast in a very amusing speech. About five the happy couple slipped away to change into their 'going away' outfits. As six o'clock, the official time of departure, approached everyone crowded into the hall and around the carriage. Sharp at six a great cheer went up as the young couple descended the stair. Much confetti and rice was thrown but it did not deter their progress to their carriage. As they sat down the bride's mother put one foot on the carriage step to give her daughter a final kiss and just at that same moment the huntsman blew the 'Gone away'. The carriage horses plunged forward and the mother was sent flying, catching her dress in the step. She was dragged by her skirt for some yards before the coachman could stop the horses. Fortunately, the lady of the manor was little hurt except in her dignity and her dress. She was rushed inside by her husband and plied with champagne. Regrettably, this did not restore her confidence and she retired upstairs, sending for her daughter Mary. It was not long before Mary reappeared and announced that her mother had retired to bed and had asked her to take her place for the rest of the evening.

The wedding invitation had included one for a dance to be held the same evening in the Hall. Most of the guests had organised house parties for dinner before returning for the dance. There were a few who came from further away who were invited to the Hall for dinner. Great was the activity as all the additional guests were found shared accommodation in which to change for dinner and the dance. Dinner was to be served in the marquee as the rest of the house was required for the dance. When they assembled for dinner it was announced that the Colonel would not be attending the dinner and dance but would be keeping his wife company upstairs and that Arthur would take his place. So Arthur and Mary were to be host and hostess and a very handsome couple they made, Mary in a beautiful cream ball gown and Arthur in his military uniform. However it was not these two who caught everyone's attention, but Mary and Ben McKenzie: Mary, tall and slim in a white dress with a tartan sash and Ben, six foot two in his dress kilt and jacket. They made a really stunning pair. Reg after his dancing experience in Scotland was less inhibited about asking girls to dance and he soon had a full programme. His small talk had improved greatly and he had no little success with the girls, much to his gratification.

Next morning, most of the house guests took their leave, but the following were staying for a further few days. General Mount, a cousin of Colonel Win-Wantock. Although now well into his seventies, he was a bachelor, tall, slim with a large white moustache and very little hair, and a great favourite with all generations. He was a keen racing man, a steward of the Jockey Club, and always full of fun. There was a soldier friend of Arthur's, the Plumb family and the McKenzies. Mrs Win-Wantock appeared for lunch and apart from a sore elbow appeared little the worse for her experience. In the afternoon Arthur organised some tennis. It must be admitted that the standard was not high as most of the players had little or no previous experience. Nevertheless, it did provide some exercise.

Reg invited the Oliver family to join the party for dinner after which the younger generation played charades. The General was appointed judge and caused much amusement in delivering his comments on each of the actors. After all this excitement life slipped into a more normal routine until it was time for him to set off on his trip to Scotland. Once more, he had arranged to spend a night in London with the Plumbs. He was embarrassed by the amount of his luggage. In addition to his usual kit he had all the fishing things his father had lent him.

Reg, who was always very punctual, reported to the station hotel in good time. He was asked to wait as Mr Wilson had not yet arrived. When he did arrive he was not hard to spot as he was carrying fishing rods and was followed by a porter with a barrow with even more luggage than he himself had. Uncle Sam was a short well built man and was dressed in his best Scottish tweeds. As soon as he saw Reg he walked straight over to him, saying, 'You must be young Win-Wantock.'

'Yes, Sir,' replied Reg and they shook hands.

'It is not hard to guess what we are off to do,' he said as he spotted Reg's fishing rods beside him. 'Come on, we had better go and find this train.'

The porter stacked all their things onto the one barrow and off they went. As they watched the porter stow the baggage in the van, Uncle Sam said, 'I always like to see it put in the right van as I have been caught by it being put in the wrong one before.'

Once seated in their first class compartment, Uncle Sam, who spoke in a somewhat abrupt manner, addressed Reg as follows. 'Do you know my big brother?'

'No, Sir, I only know Robin, I am at school with him.'

Sam continued, 'He is the head of the family, he is the one who works hard, he is the one who makes all the money, I am the one who just spends it. When I left school I started in our London office. I did not like the office life and I did not like the social life either. I had not been at this very long when my father died, at quite a young age, and I found myself heir to quite a considerable fortune. I made my peace with my brother, left the office and set off for Canada. I liked the outdoor life and I became what might be described as a kind of amateur explorer and hunter.'

Reg became more and more enthralled listening to his tales. He would describe how he would join some kindred spirit and off they would go on some hunting or fishing expedition.

Suddenly, Sam stopped. 'I am talking far too much, tell me something about yourself.'

Reg started by describing his home, his family and of course the wedding. This led to Reg inquiring into the Wilson family history. He learnt that Uncle Sam's forebears had been traders in carpets. They had bought carpets from very many small producers and had sold them in the big cities and of course in London. This had led to their importing carpets from the continent and from the far east.

This business had flourished and they had expanded into many other lines of wholesaling. Reg found it difficult to follow all the various activities in which the Wilson empire now traded. This was a side of life which he had not encountered before. Uncle Sam proved to have a nice sense of humour and he told many stories against himself.

Before they knew where they were the day had gone and they were in Glasgow. Having recovered their baggage and the necessary transport they made their way to the docks. They were shown their cabins and were told that they would not be sailing for another two hours, just nice time for dinner. Their enquiries produced the information that there were a number of places where they could dine not too far away. They decided to walk and as they set off Uncle Sam warned Reg to hang onto his wallet, saying, 'I have had quite a bit of experience of dockland areas.'

After dining and wining almost too well for Reg, they returned to the ship and turned in. Reg was accustomed when going to bed just to shut his eyes and drift off to sleep. Tonight his head was reeling, partly because of a little too much wine but more so as the result of all the new experiences he had learnt of during the day. How long he lay like that he will never know but he was woken by a rap on his door and Uncle Sam's voice saying, 'I am going up to the saloon for breakfast, join me there.'

'Thank you Sir,' was all he could think of as a reply. After a quick wash he started for the saloon and as he went he discovered that the ship was tied up alongside in Fort William.

'Sleep well? It was a nice smooth passage.'

'I am afraid I don't know; I think you must have dined me a little too well last night.'

'Never mind, the fresh air will soon put you to rights.'

After a good breakfast they left the ship to find Robert, the

Wilsons' footman, waiting to meet them.

'Good morning, Robert, nice to see you again.'

'Good morning, Sir, I trust you had a good journey. Madam has asked me to do a little shopping for her; would it be in order if I left you at the hotel while I completed these little tasks?'

'There is no need for that, we shall walk to the hotel and wait for you there. We shall leave the baggage in your charge.'

'Very good, Sir, I will be as quick as I can,' and they parted.

As they walked up the street they looked in the shop windows which gave them subjects for conversation. When they reached a fishing tackle shop Uncle Sam shot inside, declaring that he required a few new flies. Reg was fascinated with the huge selection of beautiful flies, all of different sizes and colours and all of them with such wonderful names, for instance 'thunder and lightning' and 'black doctor'. Uncle Sam, having selected a few, put them into two little piles saying, 'Those are yours and these mine and we will see who catches the most fish.' He paid the bill and they left the shop with Reg's packet firmly in his pocket.

'Thank you, Sir, that was very generous of you.'

Once at the hotel they did not have long to wait for Robert. The coachman had fed and watered the pony while Robert had been shopping and they set off at a brisk pace for home, a journey which Reg learnt would take all of three hours. The time passed quickly as Uncle Sam plied Reg with information about the country and the people who lived in it. It was obvious that he had been here many times before. Various exchanges passed between Uncle Sam and Robert on who were staying at the Lodge and who had already been and gone. Eventually, they turned off the public road and Reg learnt that they only had a further two more miles to go.

Then, all of a sudden, there it was a fairly large two-storey

Victorian stone-built house, probably not more than thirty years old. It stood in the centre of lawns with one or two not very old trees planted near by. As they drew up at the door Robin came out and welcomed his uncle of whom he was obviously very fond. Having done this he called to Reg to follow him into the house. Uncle Sam received a great welcome from Robin's two young sisters aged about twelve and fourteen while his mother, a tall lady dressed in highland tweeds, came forward to greet Reg.

'You must be famished, we have been waiting lunch,' and after a quick wash they were ushered into the dining-room.

Reg said little at lunch but listening, learnt all that had been going on on hill and river. He discovered that Mrs Wilson had caught two salmon and that her husband and Uncle George her brother had each shot a stag.

Lunch over, Mrs Wilson announced, 'I suggest you two boys go down to the river. I am going to have a rest. I shall probably come down to the river for an hour before dinner. Duncan is available to help Reg if he requires it.'

'I certainly do, Mrs Wilson, this is a new venture for me.'

They found Duncan waiting outside and they set off to walk to the river. Robin carried his own rod which was already up and ready for fishing. Duncan carried all Reg's gear. As they walked Reg explained that all his things were his father's and that he must take great care of them. 'I have never fished for salmon before.'

'That's all right, Sir, we will soon have you casting a pretty fly.'

On arriving at the river, which was quite narrow, a typical west highland stream, Robin said he would take the lower water and off he strode. Duncan, unpacking Reg's things, explained to Reg as he did so what he was doing and why. Reg had many questions to ask. Once everything was ready Duncan gave a little demonstration of how to cast and then handed over to Reg who, after one or two rather disastrous efforts, began to get the feel of what was required. By the time they had fished the first pool down, Reg was beginning to throw quite a good line. Duncan suggested that they should fish it down again using a longer line and thereby covering more of the better water. The magical feel of that good cast was beginning to grip Reg and he fished on with increasing enthusiasm.

Suddenly, Duncan, who was standing just downstream of him, said, 'Did you see that fish follow your fly round?'

'No,' he replied.

'Well, you try a few more casts before you move, he may come again.'

The next cast was a good one, that must do it, but nothing came. The next one was not so good and he was just going to lift the fly when he felt a slight tug. Duncan had warned him not to strike, 'It's too easy to pull it away, just let him hook himself.' Almost immediately the point of his rod was pulled down and the line was being pulled out.

'Keep your rod up,' said Duncan, 'and if the pressure eases, reel in.'

Reg's heart was pounding now, especially each time his fish made one of those wild dashes. On one occasion it leapt right out of the water and Reg was sure it must get off. After a while he managed to reel it in quite close to him but still he could not see it. After one or two more rushes he noticed his fish just under the surface.

'He is tiring,' said Duncan, 'it won't be long before we can net him.'

Off he went again but not so far this time.

'Oh dear,' thought Reg, 'will I ever get it on the bank,' then he noticed the fish's snout almost out of the water.

'Bring him round here,' said Duncan as he positioned himself some eight yards downstream. 'Slowly now,' he went on as he slipped the net quietly under the fish and then there he was in the net. Reg gave a huge sigh of relief as Duncan announced, 'A fine seven-pound fresh-run cock fish; well done, Sir. You will now ken what to do next time.'

Having laid the fish under some bracken in the shade they fished the next pool down. As Reg reeled in his line, Duncan said, 'I'll need to go back now for the Lady, she will no need to be kept waiting.'

They walked back to meet Mrs Wilson and Uncle Sam as they arrived at the river, each carrying a rod.

As they approached, Mrs Wilson called out, 'How did you get on, Duncan?'

'He did very well, Madam, the young gentleman will make a right good fisherman.'

'Did you enjoy yourself, Reg?'

'Yes, rather, Duncan is such a good teacher; it was wonderful.'

At that moment Uncle Sam noticed the fish lying under the bracken and picking it up, said, 'Look at this!' and the whole story came out.

'Come on, Reg,' said Uncle Sam, 'you leave your things there and we will walk on and see how Robin has been getting on.'

As they walked, Reg said, 'I caught that fish on one of your flies, Sir.'

'Don't call me Sir, just call me Uncle Sam; I am used to that.'

Quite soon they met Robin walking back saying, 'I only saw one fish all afternoon, how did you get on?'

'You will need to get a lesson from Reg, he will show you how to catch fish,' replied Uncle Sam.

The two boys sat down to watch Uncle Sam fish and of course the whole story had to come out again. No more fish were caught that afternoon.

Mr Wilson was taller than his brother, a little more formal but kindness itself to Reg and made him feel very much at home. After dinner the girls went to bed and the boys played whist with the others. Before retiring, Uncle Sam invited Reg to accompany him to the hill next day, saying, 'You had better see what goes on before you have a go yourself.' This offer was quickly accepted.

Next morning at breakfast, Uncle Sam, turning to Reg said, 'Where is the wind today?'

Reg was a little bewildered by this question and replied, 'What do you mean? Do you mean where is it blowing from?'

'Yes, the direction of the wind is the most important thing in deer stalking; it determines the whole day's strategy.'

Robin volunteered the information that the wind was still in the south-west and would be very suitable for the Glenlilt beat. 'The beat is about four miles west of here and is stalked by Jock Cameron who lives up there with his mother.'

Waiting outside they found two gillies and two ponies with one pony-man. The gentlemen were asked if they wished to ride up to Jock Cameron's. Both declined, not relishing the rather uncomfortable deer saddles. The walk was not arduous, being flat and on a gravel road. As they walked they talked and Reg learnt that the Wilsons' father had built the present lodge when the brothers were boys and that they had been coming up ever since. Jock, who had obviously seen them coming, was waiting for them. He was a well built young man dressed in a smart plus-four suit with deer-stalker hat to match. Each stalker received a new suit and cap each year. Uncle Sam moved round to the door of the house from where a small grey-haired lady emerged.

'Good morning, Mr Sam, it is nice to see you back.' After a few more words had passed between them she said, 'You won't forget to come in for your cup of tea before you walk home.'

When Uncle Sam rejoined them, Jock said, 'I have had a good look at the ground with my glass and there is nothing low down. I saw one small bunch of hinds who have now gone over the ridge but they will not bother us; they will be well below us.'

The plan was to walk to the top and then work west along the top. They set off up a pony path with Jock leading followed by Uncle Sam, Reg, a gillie carrying the rifle and the second gillie carrying the lunch bag. Before leaving Jock instructed the pony-man to wait where he was till 11.30 and then move up to a pony pit where he was to wait until he either got a signal or heard a shot. It was obvious that each man knew what part he had to play.

As they climbed, more and more ground would come into view and Jock would stop and with his glass, spy the ground to ensure they did not walk into deer unexpectedly. Reg did not find the walk up too hard. It was a nice fine day and there was a good breeze blowing which kept them cool. Once on the top Jock took the rifle from the gillie and removing it from its cover he explained to Reg that he was going to load it with five rounds but that he would not put a bullet up the breach just in case of an accident. He replaced the rifle in its cover and slung it on his shoulder, saying to Reg, 'You stay with the lads, they will keep you right.'

Although no further words passed it was clear that the 'lads' understood as he joined them. The little party set off again with the lads keeping about seven yards behind the leaders. The going was very good, almost like walking on a soft carpet of moss. They moved forward in single file with Reg between the gillies. Suddenly, the leaders stopped, turned half left and started forward step by step, clearly looking very carefully ahead of them. They stopped again and got down onto their knees and crawled forward to a large rock. Mac, the leading gillie, explained to Reg that that rock was a regular spy point from which you could see most of the corrie. After some time during which they had obviously studied the ground very carefully they crawled back out and continued on their way. Mac explained that they might well have seen deer and had decided on how the stalk should proceed.

The wind was now getting quite strong and much colder. On rounding the top they came on a small gully cutting through the top of the hill. They turned left and followed down the gully but it was not long before the leaders stopped again. Down onto their knees they got and crawled forward. They had another look and then signalling to Mac to stay where he was, they crawled on out of sight. Mac explained that they would have a short open bit of ground to cover before regaining good cover in the burn below. All their conversation was in a whisper.

'How long will we be here?' inquired Reg.

'I don't know, I have seen us sit for over an hour sometimes.'

They discussed all aspects of stalking and after a while decided to eat their lunch as it was after one o'clock. Suddenly, about 1.45, a shot shattered the quietness. Mac got up and crawling forward to where they had last seen the others, he gazed over the top. He gradually raised himself up until finally he was standing full height. After a moment he beckoned to the others to follow. Reg, who was both cold and stiff, was delighted to move. As he joined Mac he could see well below Uncle Sam and Jock standing beside the dead stag. As they made their way down the steep face Reg noticed that Mac was carrying the lunch bag and that Tom had left them.

'Where has Tom gone?' he asked.

'He has gone to fetch the ponies, he will be able to see them from that ridge,' and looking up he saw Tom almost over the ridge on their left.

By the time they reached the stag Jock had finished the grallach. Uncle Sam took the lunch bag from Mac and taking out the whisky flask offered Jock a dram before taking one himself. They stood around while Uncle Sam and Jock ate their lunch and during the chat that followed Reg learnt that Jock was glad to get that stag; he was an old beast and going back. Lunch did not take long and Jock instructed Tom, who had rejoined the party after he had loaded the stag, to bring the second pony on to the usual place as they were going to cut out and see if there was anything in the next corrie. When they left, the ponies were only a few hundred yards away. They climbed up the side of the corrie, heading for the high ground as they went. After about half an hour they started working their way round the shoulder, slowly making good the ground in front of them. It soon became apparent that there was nothing close in. They sat down and Jock spied all the far ground, not because he intended to go there but just because he wished to know what was there. This done he announced that there wasn't time to go further and they set off for home.

The walk down was easy and it was not long before they were back at the cottage. Uncle Sam and Reg were given their cup of tea and scone and jam in the 'room' while the others were given theirs in the kitchen. Having thanked Mrs Cameron for her hospitality and said goodnight to Jock, they started their walk home.

'Uncle Sam, how far away was the stag when you left us and began to crawl?'

'Six or seven hundred yards away, I should think. We had a short bit of open ground to cover before we got into the cover of the burn. At that distance and being above you can usually make it if you are careful and never move when there is a head up. They were just too far out from the burn for a shot so we had quite a difficult crawl to get within shot. I am not prepared to take chance shots at long range; that is not good stalking. You hear some chaps bragging about having shot a stag at some ridiculous range, four or five hundred yards. I wonder how many they wound. A good stalker will always get to a range where he is fairly certain of a kill; if he can't he will not shoot.'

Reg learnt a lot more about stalking during that walk home.

As it was not too late they looked into the deer larder before returning to the lodge. The ponyman had unloaded the stag and was waiting to take over the second pony. Mac and Tom soon had the stag inside and up it went on the tackle to be weighed. The weight was 14st. 6 lbs. It was dropped onto a specially shaped table and the skinning commenced. Reg was amazed at the speed everything happened. In moments the head and feet were off and the skin was being peeled from the body. This revealed just where the bullet had struck. It had been a good shot right through the ribs and into the heart.

Back in the lodge they had nice time for a hot bath and change before dinner. At dinner Reg learnt that although Robin and his parents had all had a go on the river no fish were caught. He also learnt that Robin and Donald Campbell, the head stalker, had taken the small bore rifle and gone in search of a roe buck. These could sometimes be found in the evening emerging from the birch woods into the fields. In this they were unsuccessful but they had seen some black game or black grouse as they are sometimes called. After dinner they played cards.

The next day was Sunday so there would be no sporting activities. As it was a nice day Mr Wilson decided that they would all walk to the Church. The family were all members of the Church of England but as there was no Episcopal Church in the area they attended the local Church of Scotland where they always received a great welcome from the Rev. McLelland, the minister. The church was some two miles distant so forty minutes were allowed for the journey. On arrival the ladies proceeded to take their seats while the men stayed outside and passed the time of day with their counterparts. Most of the men were stalkers, gillies or other local employees from the neighbouring estates. Mr Wilson and Sam found one such owner and exchanged news with him while the boys talked to the others. At the correct moment the church bell was rung and the men took their seats. Robin had warned Reg that the service was very different to that which they were accustomed to at home. Inside the building was very different and one thing which particularly interested Reg was that there was no music. The singing was led by a gentleman called a precentor. On the announcement of a psalm he stood up and, striking a tuning fork on the pew in front, he sang the first line to indicate the tune. He then struck his tuning fork again and this time the congregation all joined in. My readers would not wish me to linger too long on the many other differences but Reg was struck by the obvious sincerity of the congregation. After the service some ten minutes were taken to exchange welcomes with other worshippers before they walked home for lunch. In the afternoon the family walked round and called on the wives of some of the hill staff.

The plan for Monday was for Mr Wilson and Robin to go up with Jock Cameron, Mrs Wilson and Uncle Sam to fish which left Reg to have some target practice with Donald Campbell and if all went well to have a short day on the home beat. All did go well and Reg proved a good shot. On returning to the gunroom there was an elderly man waiting with a pony. Turning to Reg Donald said, 'This is Willie McRae, he has a croft just down the road and he comes with his own pony to help us out whiles.'

Having shaken Willie by the hand Reg and his little party set off up the hill path. After about half an hour they approached the top of a ridge. From here Donald slowed down, making good the near ground as more and more came into view. As soon as he could get a clear view of the hill in front Donald sat down and taking out his telescope, began to study the ground. Reg thought he could see a bunch of deer on a green patch some considerable distance ahead.

After some time Donald took his glass down and addressing Reg, said, 'You will be seeing the deer on the green, well, they are all hinds but there are some stags lying further up in the heather. There could be a shootable beast with them. What did you see, Willie?'

'I saw the hinds and the stags but I think I saw a single beast walking up well below the stags. I can't see him now, he must either have lain down or gone out of sight.'

'Well, we will leave you here, Willie, while we go round and see what's in the stags.'

They slipped back behind the ridge and set off to the right. As they climbed they kept the shoulder between them and the deer, but this exposed them to fresh ground to their right. Suddenly Donald stopped, he had obviously seen something. Reg being a foot or so lower down could not see what it was. Slowly, Donald bent his knees until he was out of sight of what he saw.

He took a step down and said to Reg, 'I saw a hind's head not too far ahead; you wait there and I will have a little look and see what's in it.'

Putting down the rifle he crawled out to the left to another vantage point. Reg's heart began to beat a little faster as he wondered what was going on. Donald crawled back and said, 'It's just a hind and calf, we will have to move them. I think they will go down and not bother us any more.'

On that he stood up and slowly moved up. There was a bark, or what Reg learnt later was a hind bark, and the hind trotted off with her calf to the right and down the hill. Donald waited until she was out of sight and then continued up the hill.

After they had climbed for some time, Donald stopped and turning, said, 'I am just going to have a wee look from here,' and he started walking very carefully to his left, one step at a time. After a very short pause he bent down and returned to Reg. 'They're all there still, but they are too far out. We'll gang a wee bit further round yet.'

When this happened a second time, Donald did not return to Reg but sank down onto his knees and signalled to Reg to crawl in and join him. They crawled forward together with Reg not daring to look up. When they stopped Reg noticed that Donald was gazing ahead so he too lifted his head ever so slowly until he could see over the little ridge in front of them. There, not more than 120 yards away, the stags were lying.

'Follow me,' Donald whispered and lying flat down started edging forward on his elbows with his head down. Reg followed Donald's boots. When after some time Donald stopped Reg looked up and found that they had crossed the first ridge and were in a little hollow completely hidden from the deer. Donald, who had the rifle half out of its cover, removed it altogether and signalled to Reg to come alongside him. Putting the rifle on the ground in front of him, he whispered, 'We should get a shot from here.'

He started edging forward and indicated to Reg to do likewise. 'When you push the rifle forward, mind you keep the muzzle out of the heather.'

Reg soon realised that the top of their heads must be in view of the deer. 'Get yourself comfortable for a shot,' he heard in a whisper. After a bit of manoeuvring, he indicated that he was ready.

'Do you see the one lying on the left? Take that one when he gets up. You can lower the rifle until he gets up but don't shoot until I say so.'

As Reg watched he thought his neck would break. He just had to rest his chin on the butt of the rifle.

'I think he is going to rise, Sir,' so Reg slowly raised the rifle and sure enough the stag got up and stood looking directly away from the two. He sniffed the ground, took two steps forward and sniffed another stag. He then shook himself and walked away out of sight. Reg's heart sank as Donald indicated to him to slide back.

'The others are all young stags, we will need to try again from above.'

There followed a long slow crawl back over the ridge. Once back, Reg had to admit it was nice to stand up and have a stretch. They walked on up the hill until it was obvious they must be well above the herd. Donald then started looking over the crest to locate them. Quite soon he pointed down below then turned and bending down set off to the right. By clever use of the ground they got quite well down and in behind a good ridge. As they crawled up and looked over there was nothing to be seen. Reg heard a whisper say, 'They are just round the corner grazing, this way, just get yourself comfortable for a shot.'

Almost immediately a young stag walked into view really quite close. 'There he comes now, Sir,' whispered Donald, 'Wait a wee minute; he will come closer.' After what seemed an age Reg heard,

'Take him now, Sir.'

Reg held his breath and squeezed. Bang! The stag took a little jump in the air and ran off.

'Good shot, Sir, you have got him,' and there he was standing, he wobbled and fell over dead. The remainder, who had bunched together when the shot was fired, stood watching. When the stag fell they trotted off.

'I like to let them go quietly and not show myself,' Donald explained.

Once they were out of sight they got up and walked down to their stag. Before Donald started the gralloch he took out his glass saying, 'I will just have a look and see if Willie has seen us. Yes he has, he is well on his way already.'

Once the gralloch was completed, Donald picked up the rifle and handing it to Reg, said, 'It will not be ill to drag him down a bit if you would not mind taking the rifle.' Thereupon he put himself within the antlers and taking one in each hand set off down the hill at such a pace Reg could not keep up. After a very considerable distance he stopped and as Reg rejoined him he said, 'Willie will get in here all right,' and when he looked down there was Willie quite close.

Reg was looking forward to watching how they secured the stag on the pony. The first thing they did was to tighten the girths to ensure the saddle did not slip, then Willie took the hind end and Donald the head and they lifted it and pushed the hindquarters over the saddle until it was approximately balanced. The next move was to pass a strap between the forelegs and secure it to the saddle. A similar strap secured the hindquarters and finally a third strap secured the head. Willie adjusted the straps to ensure the load was properly balanced and off he set for home.

It is difficult to describe in words how with only three straps a dead stag can be secured on the back of a pony. It is amazing what rough ground a pony can cross with its load. It is not easy to walk side by side down a hill but whenever this was possible Reg discussed every move they had made that day. He learnt that it was an old stag whose head was 'going back'. It was a nine pointer and weighed 15 stone 2 lbs. When they arrived at the larder there was no sign of the other party having returned.

Back in the lodge Reg received many congratulations from his hostess and from Uncle Sam, but the two who really wanted to hear all about his success were the two girls. After all, they were not all that much younger than he was but they had never been given the opportunity to accompany a stalking party. Reg said to the girls, 'Would you really like to go out with a stalking party?'

'Yes! Yes!' they both exclaimed.

'Well, you leave it to me and I will see what I can do.'

It was not long before Robin and his father returned from the hill. Robin too had been successful shooting his first stag of that season and his third stag in total.

At dinner that night Mr Wilson announced that Uncle Sam would be going out with Jock Cameron and that he would be going to the home beat. 'Sir,' said Reg, addressing Mr Wilson, 'Would it be possible for the girls and me to go with you, they have promised me that they would be very quiet and if they get tired I could bring them home.'

This suggestion sent all tongues wagging, and all sorts of reasons were put forward against the proposal. All were silenced when Mrs Wilson announced that she thought it was a very kind thought of Reg and she said to her husband, 'You would not mind, would you?'

Having got this far the girls spent the rest of the evening making their plans with their mother. Next morning the girls, known as H and E (Helen and Elizabeth), were down early for breakfast, determined that there should be no excuse to leave them behind. The party consisted of Mr Wilson, Donald, Mac, Willie with his pony, Reg and the two girls. They were so excited, they had never accompanied a stalking party before and this time they had been invited by a boy. As they set off Reg warned them that if they could not keep up he would have to take them home. They followed a different path to that taken by Reg and Donald yesterday. They walked in single file with only Willie and the pony behind them. All went well until they came to a steep section where the young ladies were quickly in trouble, they slipped and slithered all over the place. Their boots, although of adequate weight, were not fitted with any tackits to prevent slipping. Fortunately, this steep section was short and they were soon back on a more manageable gradient. They plodded on until after about an hour's climbing Donald and his father sat down to have a spy. This provided a very welcome opportunity for the young ladies to rest and few words passed between the young people. After about ten minutes their father came back and explained that they had seen some stags and would leave Willie and the pony here and begin their stalk. Reg explained to him the difficulty the girls were having with their unsuitable footwear and suggested that they might wait with Willie and that if it got too cold they could walk home. This was accepted and Donald, Father, and Mac commenced their stalk. This gallant action by Reg came as a great relief to the girls who were finding great difficulty in keeping up.

Willie suggested that they should move into a more sheltered spot.

'I always sit here for an hour or so, then I take a little look to see how they are getting on.'

The time passed quite quickly, Willie had lots of stories as did

Reg. The girls were quite happy just to pop in the odd question, it was such a novelty to them. Willie's stories got more and more impossible and they began to realise that he was pulling their legs, which led to much laughter. Reg too enjoyed teasing the girls who really enjoyed it although they pretended not to.

'I'll just have a wee look,' said Willie as he got up and walked over to where Donald had been spying. He returned, saying, 'The deer have moved up a little but they should manage them there; we will just have to wait a wee bit longer.'

They were taking turns in looking through Willie's telescope when they heard a shot. Willie was back in the spy position in seconds, looking to see the outcome.

'I've got them, they have got their beast all right, I will have to be going.'

Collecting the pony he set off up the path. Reg suggested to the girls that they should start for home so that they could take their time and not risk falling and breaking a leg. It took them a long time to get down but they made it before the stalking party. As they walked down, Reg learnt for the first time that there were two more children, a girl of eight and a boy of six left in England with Nannie, the under nurse and the housekeeper.

Uncle Sam too had a good day but their mother and Robin had a blank on the river. The next day the weather broke and the mist came down and the rain poured down. Nobody ventured out, the day was spent playing family games. It gave Reg a chance to get up to date with his journal.

By the next morning the rain had stopped and there was great expectations that all that rain would have improved the fishing. The total fishing available was two short beats and the plan was for Uncle Sam and Duncan to go to one and the two boys go together to the other beat. When this plan was announced at breakfast H turned to her mother and said, 'Can we go with the boys?'

'You had better ask them,' she replied.

'Can we come with you?' asked the two girls.

'I suppose so,' replied Robin, while Reg replied, 'Yes.'

On arriving at the river the boys tossed for who should start and Robin won. 'Have you never fished, H?' enquired Reg.

'Not really, I have had a little go with Father's small rod but I never caught anything.'

'Have a cast on the grass with my rod,' and Reg got up and prepared it. In the meantime E went off with Robin. H got on well on the grass so it was agreed that she would have a go once Robin had moved down. That moment came quite soon and with Reg as her gillie she made a start. All was going well when there was a crack behind and the fly was gone. Reg replaced the fly and refused to take over the rod. H was beginning to get tired and was preparing to hand over to Reg when suddenly there was a splash in the water and down went the point of the rod. Reg, with his own triumph fresh in his mind, carefully instructed the young lady on how to play the fish. H had of course witnessed her mother and father catching fish, but this was quite a new experience. Reg, who was almost as nervous as his young pupil, became even more so when he realised that E had taken the landing net. He had heard about people tailing a fish but he had never seen it done. H continued to play the fish with great gentleness until at last it came to the surface and showed little life. At that juncture Reg positioned himself some five or six yards below H and called to H to pull the fish over to him and try and run it up the bank. As the fish reached the bank Reg jumped into the shallow water and seized it by the tail with both hands. In his anxiety to get it on the bank he stumbled but managed to throw the fish onto the bank before landing on his hands and knees in the river. By the time he was back on dry land H had put the rod down and dispatched the poor creature with a stone. 'Well done!' he said as he came up to her. She in her turn was so excited she threw her arms round his neck and gave him a huge hug. The playing of that fish had taken a very long time and they were just sorting out their gear when Robin and E returned carrying a fish in the net. The heavy rain of yesterday had certainly brought some fresh fish up the river. It was now time to return home for lunch where the fish weighed in at four and a half pounds for H's and five for Robin's. When Reg came down from changing his wet clothes Uncle Sam had returned with a seven pounder.

In the afternoon they swopped beats and Mrs Wilson accompanied Uncle Sam. No more fish were caught although they fished hard. Mr Wilson got a stag. So, great was the rejoicing at dinner that evening. There was however, a tinge of sadness, especially in the heart of one young lady, as Reg was to start for home next day.

Next morning Robin and Uncle Sam went to the hill while Reg wrote up his journal and packed up. He was to catch the post bus at midday which would return him to Fort William in time to catch the night boat to Glasgow.

Chapter 3

Reg arrived back in London after a dull and uneventful journey. As usual, he took a cab to the Plumbs' where he was always welcome. When his cousins saw the stag's antlers they could not wait to hear his story. However, as the dinner hour was fast approaching his uncle decided that the exchange of holiday experiences must wait. It was quite late that evening before these exchanges were completed.

Reg returned home to a very quiet household. All traces of the wedding had gone, Mary was staying away and only his parents were at home. They were delighted to hear of his days on the hill and the river and that he had been so successful. He handed back his father's fishing equipment augmented by the extra flies given to him by Uncle Sam. To his surprise his father said, 'You can keep all that gear, I don't think I shall ever fish again.'

'Thank you very much,' replied Reg, 'but we can share it.'

'Very good, that's what we will do.'

He spent the next few days writing up his journal and walking round the estate catching up with all the staff and what they had been doing. Life was quiet and he was delighted to accept an invitation to lunch with the Olivers. As always, he received a great welcome from the twins. They were thrilled to hear all about his highland holiday. When he came to recounting the story of

Helen's fish they both shouted out, 'I wish that had been me! I would love to catch a salmon!' They, in their turn, had much to tell him about what had been going on on the farm, a subject in which they now took great interest. Great was his surprise when they informed him that next month Ann was going to a hospital to learn nursing and Isobel to a college to study teaching.

'What shall I do about the reports on the farm?' he asked.

'Daddy will have to do that, we will tell him,' and laughing they said, 'you know what that means.'

Before returning home he said, 'I hope you will both find time for the occasional letter.'

'Oh yes, we will.'

He paid visits to some of his hunting friends and before long it was time to return to school.

Back at school Reg found himself in the top form. This was going to be quite a challenge and in addition he was determined to prepare for the university exams at the end of the year. Just before he had left for school his father had informed him that he was going to give him a cash allowance which would have to meet all his expenses except for his clothes and his education but he had not named a sum.

During the term he received three letters of special significance. The first was from his father informing him that he had opened a bank account in his name and had deposited a sum of money there. This sum would be repeated each quarter. The sum deposited seemed generous to Reg and he did not anticipate any difficulty living within his means. The second letter was an invitation to spend Christmas with the Plumbs, to attend a dance which they were giving and to be one of their party for one or two other parties.

The third letter was from Olga inviting him to stay with her and John for a shoot at Bush Hall, John's father's place in January. 'Ask Father if you can bring keeper John and a dog with you. He would be a help to you and a great help picking up. We can put him up.' As Mary had decided to stay in Paris for Christmas these invitations were especially welcome. He had also received letters from Ann and Isobel. The one from Ann was much the most interesting as it described in graphic detail much of her hospital life.

He returned home for a few days at the end of term during which time he obtained his father's permission to take John with him to the shoot. When informed, John was thrilled at the idea as he had never been out of the district.

Reg always enjoyed his visits to the Plumbs. Uncle William was a great joker and he had handed this characteristic down, especially to Susan, the eldest girl. The Plumbs as a family were short, broad and jolly. Peter, Susan and to a lesser extent Rosemary were, like himself, growing up and developing a much more adult attitude to life.

Reg while in the train to London was racking his brain as to what to get his cousins for Christmas. He now had funds, so on his arrival in town he set off for the shops. As he gazed into one window he saw theatrical make up. He popped in and emerged some time later with a variety of things suitable for both males and females. He arrived home and subsequently, with the aid of Aunt Jane, who never asked what was in the various boxes, he got them all wrapped. His choice proved a great success and much fun was had with them over the festive season.

Reg, who had grown into a very handsome young man, was in much demand at the dance, all the girls wanted to dance with him. Quite early in the evening Susan came to him and said, 'Reg, I am going to introduce you to Pamela. She is an awful snob and fancies herself. She is good looking but very boring.'

Reg replied, 'I will ask her to dance some time ahead and when the time comes put on some disguise and see if she recognises me. If so, well and good, if not I will say, "Oh! I am sorry, there must be another girl who looks just like you," and leave her.' The trick worked and she refused him and she was left sitting without a partner while Reg danced with Susan. What a delightful time he had over that Christmas holiday, there was so much fun and laughter.

He arrived home in time for his father's New Year shoot. This was a much more staid affair as Arthur was not available and all the guests were his parents' friends. His father was slowing down considerably and he found himself left to do quite a lot of the organising. He enjoyed the challenge and the much lower tempo of life. This little bit of responsibility made him realise just how fortunate he was to have been born into this affluent society where there were staff and servants everywhere to carry out one's every requirement. The shoot went well, the weather was good and everyone enjoyed their two days. When it was all over and the guests were departing several of them complimented him on the efficient way he had organised everything.

Another bit of organising which now required his attention was his visit to the Goodhos. They lived some hundred miles away and there was no convenient railway available. He wrote to Olga asking her if she could arrange accommodation for a carriage, two horses and a man. He planned to take two days, stopping off for the night in a provincial town where there were several inns. In the meantime he managed to get two days hunting before setting off for the shoot.

The journey started well and he found very nice night accommodation and he booked in again for his return trip.

Having received detailed instructions from Olga they found no difficulty finding the house, especially as they completed the journey before dark. The house was not large but it was very comfortable and Reg found a very welcoming fire burning in his bedroom. Olga was alone, John not having returned from the shoot. Reg had been invited for the second of a two-day shoot. Olga was delighted to have Reg to herself for a little while and she began pumping him for information. She knew he had been with the Plumbs for Christmas and that he had been in the north during the summer. It was not long before John returned and it was time to change for dinner.

That evening passed very quickly, they had so much to talk about. Reg learnt that some other young people of his age had been invited for tomorrow. They had to drive a few miles to the shoot next morning but as it was bright Olga, although pregnant, decided to accompany them. Reg had shot quite well at home so he was hoping he could do so again today.

On arrival at the big house he found John with his dog waiting for him with his gun and cartridges. After a brief period of introductions they moved to the first drive. After his practice at home Reg was in even better form and John was very proud of his young gentleman. On his left he had John Goodho's uncle, a brother of his host. He was a very good shot. On the other side was a local tenant farmer who was not quite so good. Uncle William, as that was how he was introduced, was a tall thin wiry figure with a wonderful twinkle in his eye. He conversed freely with Reg during which Reg discovered that he was a retired General. Reg really enjoyed his morning, he was shooting well and everybody was so friendly.

At lunch he was placed next to a charming and most attractive young lady, probably just older than himself. He felt very flattered when she asked if she might accompany him in the afternoon. When the shoot was over Olga decided that she wished to go straight home so Reg sought out his host, to whom he had hardly spoken, and thanked him.

His host replied, 'My granddaughter Felicity tells me you are a very good shot, you must come again some time.'

He would have gladly walked home with John and his dog but felt he must go with Olga and John. On the way home Olga announced, 'I have invited Felicity and her brother Pug for dinner tonight, I thought you would enjoy that,' as she dug him in the ribs with her elbow.

'Good,' he said, feeling a little embarrassed but very pleased. They had a lovely evening playing cards at the end of which he had collected another address. He would liked to have stayed longer but he had to get home and ready for school.

The return journey started well but as they drew up at the inn there were a few flakes of snow blowing about. He awoke next morning to find some four inches of snow. Soon after they moved off it started to snow again. The poor horses were slipping with great balls of snow building up in their shoes Their pace was reduced to a walk. The coachman suggested stopping and buying some butter with which he would smear the inside of the horses' shoes to stop the snow balling. They stopped at a roadside farm and managed to buy some butter. This helped considerably but still a walk was all they could manage. They stopped for half an hour at an inn to feed and water the horses but Reg was determined to get home that night. The snow stopped and the sky cleared which greatly improved visibility and progress. They were all tired, cold and hungry by the time they got home. Reg had only one day before he had to set off back to school.

Once there he found that in addition to being head of his house, he had been appointed to other positions of authority in the school. He enjoyed this extra responsibility and the privileges which went with it. He was excused all forms of compulsory games which gave him time for several extra-mural activities. His housemaster suggested he should try for a scholarship at Cambridge, a suggestion he readily fell in with. He went home for the Easter holidays determined to work hard. He found that Mary had returned and was immersed in preparing for the forthcoming season. It was fun having her at home, she was more social and jovial than Olga. She in her turn found her brother had grown into a young man from a boy and they really enjoyed one another's company.

Ken Oliver had not written to him during the term so Reg spent quite a lot of time at the farm catching up on what had been going on. He also discovered that only Isobel was at home so he invited her down for lunch. She, separated from her sister for the first time, was growing up fast and she very much enjoyed hearing all about Mary's time in Paris. During the holidays the exciting news was received of the arrival of his first nephew. Olga had given birth to a son.

Back at school for the last time he learnt that David had decided to have a go at passing the Cambridge exam. He was captain of school cricket and was now keen to get his Blue. When the time came there were six boys who travelled to Cambridge together to sit the exam. Reg had in his pocket a letter of introduction to one of the tutors from Uncle Robert. On arrival the boys dispersed to the varying colleges of their choice but agreed to meet up again for the return journey. Reg found that he had been alloted a room in college and a gyp (a male servant) to look after him. On his arrival he had left his letter of introduction at the porter's lodge and he was sitting in his room trying to make up his mind on his next move when there was a knock on the door. It came from a middle-aged man who introduced himself as Mr Roger. 'I have just received Professor McKenzie's letter,' and they shook hands. Mr Roger said how pleased he was to meet Reg and continued to explain to him all the domestic arrangements in college and how to find the examination halls next day. They parted with Mr Roger inviting Reg to his room after dinner.

At dinner in Hall he sat next to a first year student who filled him in on what was going on and on many other useful details. Amongst other things he learnt that Mr Roger was a keen athlete. After dinner he found his way without difficulty to Mr Roger's rooms where he was introduced to two other young candidates. Having refrained from drinking alcohol at dinner Reg accepted the glass of port he was offered. They spent a very pleasant evening in general conversation and they parted wishing one another good luck next day in their exams.

He slept well and was woken next morning by his gyp who at the appropriate moment brought him his breakfast. At the examination hall he met some of his school friends and they agreed to meet for lunch. After the afternoon session he and another boy went for a walk before returning to their colleges for dinner. Such spare time as he had before and after dinner he devoted to revision. Next day, after the exams were over, he was invited to another college where one of the other boys had an elder brother in residence. There, they started to celebrate and some did this too well. Reg, who was scared of excess alcohol and of doing something which would displease his father, left the party early.

Back at school life became rather pointless, although he was still expected to do the school exams. He was informed that the scholarship results usually came out quite quickly, probably in about fourteen days. In the mail one morning he received a letter, the handwriting on the envelope he did not recognise. Great was his joy when, on opening it, he found it was from Felicity, inviting him to stay next holidays. She explained that every year they had a house party to celebrate her parents' wedding day. As by that time he would have left school he felt that he could accept this invitation without referring first to his parents. She closed her letter in these words: 'I was sorry Olga dragged you away so soon after the shoot, I was hoping for some further conversation with you. Do come.' His decision was immediate and his letter of acceptance went off next morning.

A few days later, on returning to his house one evening, he found a note in the letter rack from his house master saying that the Headmaster wished to see him. Scribbled on the bottom was 'Good News'. Reg had a very happy relationship with his housemaster but not so with the Headmaster. Although Reg, as one of the senior boys, met him frequently he always remained very remote. Next morning when he knocked on the Headmaster's study door and heard the familiar, 'Come in,' great was his surprise to find him standing up with outstretched hand and a smile on his face.

'Well done,' were his welcoming words, 'you have surpassed even our best expectations. That is one of the best results ever achieved by a boy from this school.'

Reg did not know what to say, all he could manage was, 'Thank you, Sir.' The Headmaster eased his embarrassment by saying, 'Come and sit down.'

There followed quite a long conversation during which the Head asked why he had selected that particular college. Reg then explained his relationship with Uncle Robert and that he had advised him.

'Well,' came the reply, 'with that advice available you do not require any further advice from me.'

The news soon leaked out and David was one of the first to congratulate him. From that moment on he was a school hero, almost as important as the Captain of football or cricket, but not quite.

That night he wrote a very humble but factual letter to his father. He knew how pleased he would be. He was very fond of his father.

In due time he received the following reply,

> Dear Reg, Your letter brought very welcome news. Your mother joins me in sending our congratulations. She says she cannot understand where you get the brains from.
>
> Your affectionate father.

A few weeks later he said good-bye to school for the last time. He went home with an invitation from David to stay with them in September, an invitation which he also accepted.

Chapter 4

When Reg arrived home he was alarmed to see how frail his sister Mary looked. He had not been informed of her illness in case it unsettled him during his exams. Mary had been taken ill while in London doing the season with her mother. She had been confined to bed for some time but when sufficiently recovered to travel had returned home. She said she was better but she did not look well to Reg.

That first evening after dinner Reg, who had now decided that he no longer required parental permission to go visiting, announced his plans for the holidays. He said that next week he was going to stay with Felicity Dart. Felicity, he explained, was a niece of Olga's, being the daughter of John's eldest sister. He explained that he had met her at the shoot. Then in September he was going to stay with David in Yorkshire. He was closely questioned about the Dart family. He was unable to give many details other than that Major Sir Richard Dart had been a cavalry soldier who had left the army on the death of his father and returned to manage his estates. Felicity was the eldest of six children. Reg learnt that before he returned from the Darts his brother would be home on extended leave before sailing for South Africa.

For Reg the next week was to be a hectic one. He planned to dash up to London to replace his schoolboy outfits with something more grown up. He spent one night with his cousins and spent a lot of money. Back home again he visited all the estate staff, enjoying talking to the gardeners, the keepers and the stable staff. They all liked his visits, he was very popular with them all. Finally he went to see Ken, half hoping that one or both of the twins would be at home. On that score he was unlucky but it meant that he spent more time on the farm activities.

His journey to the Darts meant his catching a train from another station somewhat further away. Once there, however, the train journey was quite short, only a little over an hour.

On arrival, he found the station to be very small and a little distance from the village. However he found a cab, the driver of which looked rather a bright young man.

'Where to?' he was asked and as soon as he replied the driver replied, 'Coming for the garden party and the cricket match are you?'

Reg replied, 'I don't know anything about a cricket match.'

'That's all right, Sir, you will be playing. I hope to be playing for the village.'

They passed through quite a small village with a nice green and on the far side entered lodge gates. The drive was about half a mile long before they drew up at the front door of a very attractive Elizabethan manor house. As he alighted from the cab he said to the cabbie, 'Don't bowl too fast at me when we next meet.'

'You are quite safe, Sir, I am the wicket keeper.'

He paid his fare and rang the bell. He was let in by a liveried footman and taken to the drawing room. There he met Lady Dart and Felicity who immediately introduced him to her mother. May Dart was a strikingly good looking woman with a wonderful figure for the mother of six. She took him warmly by the hand saying, 'I hear that you are not only a good shot but a scholar as well.'

At this he must have shown some embarrassment as Felicity came to his rescue by saying, 'Olga told me about the scholarship.'

They sat down and started to chat. He discovered that Felicity was some four years older than her nearest brother who was just fourteen, her father having been posted overseas just after she was born. There was another brother of twelve and three younger girls.

Felicity said, 'Let's go out and see what Papa is doing, I think he is with his beloved horses.'

It was a beautiful warm summer afternoon. They took a path round the side of the house which led to the stable block. Here there was stabling for ten horses but there were only four carriage horses inside. All the hunters were out at grass. They walked on what was obviously the road to the home farm. As they rounded a corner, there, in the middle of a grass park, were some five mares and foals with two men standing admiring them. As they approached Felicity called out, 'Papa, I have brought Reg to see your latest pet.'

Sir Richard came to meet them and said, 'Hello, Reg, I have heard a lot about you,' and held out his hand.

As Reg took it he replied, 'How do you do, Sir, I hope it is not all bad.'

They admired the mares and foals. The last time Reg had seen stock of this standard had been when staying with David. Sir Richard, having recounted the history and pedigree of each of the mares and the sires of the foals asked Reg when he had arrived, following this with, 'Where did you lunch?'

'I missed out on that one, Sir,' Reg replied.

'You must be hungry, come and see if we can find some afternoon tea.'

Reg enjoyed the opportunity while walking back, to have words with his host. When they entered the drawing room, there were a young lady and man talking to Lady Dart. Felicity immediately introduced them as Uncle Tom and Aunt Una.

'Uncle Tom is Papa's young brother,' she explained. 'He always comes for the match, I don't know what we would do without him.'

Uncle Tom had served in India for some time and had returned home some five years earlier to get married. He at present had a staff job and they had one small son.

At that moment Lady Dart rang the bell and when the footman appeared said, 'Tea please, Wilson.'

'Yes, my Lady,' he replied and departed.

Just then Bill and Clive, Felicity's brothers, came in. 'Had your tea, boys?' Lady Dart enquired.

'Yes, we had it in the school room, thank you.'

From that moment on there was never a quiet moment.

The boys did not appear for dinner and after dinner Felicity was instructed to produce her violin. She, with her mother at the piano, then entertained the company with a most amusing and enjoyable musical evening.

Next morning after breakfast Reg was invited to accompany Sir Richard and Uncle Tom who were going on an inspection of the horses and the farm. As they walked Reg began asking Uncle Tom about India. Tom, becoming very impressed by the very well informed questions Reg posed, asked, 'How do you know so much about India?' Reg replied by telling how he had met Miss Brough and Miss Long on the train and had subsequently read their book.

'Oh, I have heard of those two remarkable ladies but I never met them.'

Having inspected the horses they moved on to the farm. Here it was Sir Richard who was impressed by Reg's knowledge of farming. Reg explained the situation at home and his close relationship with Ken Oliver. There was little to see in the farm buildings, the stock all being out in the fields, so they walked on to watch the grain harvest being cut. As they walked the conversation inevitably drifted to field sports. By the time they returned for lunch Reg reckoned that to have been one of the more interesting mornings.

After lunch the following assembled on the lawn to play croquet, the two brothers with their wives, the two boys, Felicity and Reg. There was much leg pulling as to who should play with whom and Sir Richard turned to Reg and said, 'You seem to have the answer to most things, how do you think we should play?'

Reg had to admit that he knew nothing about croquet, never ever having seen a game. The following pairings were finally agreed: Lady Dart and Uncle Tom; Sir Richard and Clive; Felicity and Bill; and finally Aunt Una and Reg. Reg tried to do what his partner suggested but with little success. The final winners were Lady Dart and Uncle Tom as was expected.

Next day was the cricket match and Uncle Tom said to Reg, 'What is your cricket like, young man?'

'Not much better than my croquet,' was Reg's reply.

'Well, if that is the case we had better have some practice in the morning.'

It was a very happy house party with much banter. The boys, having heard that Reg was a scholar, expected a very solemn young man who probably wore glasses. They were delighted to find out how wrong they were. The evening was spent playing a variety of card games. The idea of a cricket match between the village and the Manor house had started some five years earlier on the present Sir Richard taking up residence in the Manor. The house team this year was to consist of Sir Richard, Uncle Tom, Reg and the footman Wilson from the house, the farm bailiff and two others from the estate and a tenant farmer whose party was to be three. Bill was spare man and Felicity the scorer. They were all to assemble at the Manor by noon for a sandwich lunch before proceeding to the village where the match was to be played on the green.

When they awoke next morning there had obviously been some rain.

'I hope the sun comes out and dries the pitch, we never have a good game on a wet pitch,' commented Sir Richard. The sun did come out and spirits began to rise. However, it was too wet for practice so Uncle Tom began questioning Reg on his cricket and when he learnt that he had played for his house at school he felt reassured. By 11.30 the team and their supporters had begun to arrive and the sun was shining brightly. By noon there was a great spread of food laid out on tables in front of the house. Uncle Tom, who was to captain the home side, had learnt much about the incoming local players from Wilson who himself normally played for the village side.

At one thirty Sir Richard and Uncle Tom led the team down the drive followed by a four-wheeled dray with the equipment and some of the less able ladies. As they emerged from the lodge gates they saw the opposition awaiting them outside the little wooden pavilion. The village team was captained by the schoolmaster. He and Sir Richard, having shaken hands, introduced their teams. The vicar, accompanied by his verger, who were to be the umpires, then produced a coin and according to tradition the schoolmaster called tails and tails it was. He elected to bat. Uncle Tom who was a spin bowler and Wilson who was usually the local fast bowler opened the bowling.

The first wicket fell with the score at 16. Thereafter, runs came and wickets fell till finally the last wicket fell at four fifteen with the score at 105. As the match progressed Uncle Tom suspected that Wilson was favouring some of his pals so he was replaced by a young man called Biffin who was a friend who had been brought in to make up the numbers. He proved to be deadly and most of the wickets fell to him. Reg during his short spell took one caught in the outfield.

Tea having been taken play recommenced. The batting was opened by the brothers who looked all set when Sir Richard was run out with the score at twenty. Wickets fell quickly and when Uncle Tom was caught when attempting to hit a six it looked as if they were heading for defeat. Reg came in with the score at 51 for 6. As there was still plenty of time he was determined not to throw away his wicket. They had only scored another four runs when his companion was clean bowled. In came the unknown quantity, Biffin. He walked up to Reg and said, 'It looks as if we have got to do something about this, you just stay in, I will make the runs.'

'All right,' replied Reg, thinking to himself, what wonderful confidence. Biffin was true to his word, scoring fluently all round the wicket. Reg scored the odd run now and again and so the score mounted. By the time it had reached 80 Reg's confidence was growing and he too began to score a little quicker. In the end these two put on 56 for the eighth wicket and so won the match.

When celebrating their victory in the pub it was revealed that Biffin often played for his County as a Gentleman. Reg took the opportunity to confirm with his cabbie friend that he was picking him up on Monday morning. The party did not last long as the non-resident players were keen to get back to the Manor and on their way home.

That evening he was invited to sit next his hostess. Up till then he had had little conversation with her. She had struck him as quiet and unassuming. She proved to be a very good conversationalist and they had a great discussion on a wide variety of subjects. He discovered that she was a keen rider to hounds and had won many prizes showing hunters. She had never been to Scotland and was most interested to hear about his visits to St Andrews.

After dinner when he was talking to Sir Richard, Felicity called to him, 'Come and make a four at billiards.'

Sir Richard immediately interjected, 'Off you go, I expect that you have discovered that in this house you have to do what you are told by the ladies.'

Reg was a little surprised to receive this summons as it was not usual for ladies to play billiards. Felicity's mother and Uncle Tom were to be the opposition. As he followed her he said, 'I am hopeless, we do have a table but it is seldom used.' Uncle Tom was in a class by himself and his team had their 100 up when the young ones had only scored 42.

Next morning was Sunday and at breakfast Sir Richard reminded everybody that they would be leaving early for Church as Mama was to play the organ. They formed quite a party, twelve in all, including the small children and Nanny. They were welcomed by the Vicar who gave Sir Richard and Uncle Tom details of the lessons they were to read. It was quite clear that the family played a very prominent part in the community. After Church came the family lunch at which all the children were present along with Nanny. Lunch over, Reg, the two boys and Felicity set off to walk to the fish pond. The two boys ran ahead and they did not see them again. Reg found Felicity very good company, she was both cheery and highly intelligent. They never lacked for something to talk about.

That evening the Vicar and his wife came to dinner, and as it was late before they left the table there was no time for any games. As he said good-bye next morning Lady Dart said, 'You must bring your horse over in the winter and we will show you a good pack of hounds.'

He replied, 'I would love to do that but the Christmas vacation is short,' to which Lady Dart replied, 'You write to Felicity and tell her how you're placed nearer the time.'

'Oh do come, Reg, that would be fun,' Felicity said, gripping his arm.

Back home again he told what an amusing time he had had. His mother was delighted that he was such a social success, she always thought that he was going to be one of those shy loners.

'Where is Arthur, I thought he was to be at home when I got back?'

'He and June have gone to the Knights for the night, they will be back tomorrow.'

Mary was looking better but she had hardly been out of the house since he left. He arranged that, if it was a nice day, he would take her for a drive in the trap. His mother used the pony and trap to be driven on short local visits and it was a lovely vehicle for a nice summer day. Next morning lived up to expectations so he ordered the trap for 2.00 p.m. Reg decided that he would drive and that they would not take a man. They made two calls which were much enjoyed by Mary. When they arrived home Arthur and June had returned. June made a rather late entry into the drawing room before dinner and as she did so Arthur announced, 'Here comes my bride to be.' Reg had not realised why they had gone to visit her family. They wished to announce their engagement before Arthur sailed for South Africa but they did not plan to marry until he returned. It would mean a long engagement but they both wanted it that way.

Reg had two weeks before he set off again to stay with David. During this time he took Mary on several more drives. He also had a much enjoyed lunch and afternoon with the Olivers. Both the girls were at home together for the first time. They had both blossomed and were real young ladies now. They had a great deal to talk about which led to much laughter.

As Reg prepared for his next trip he seemed to have an enormous amount of luggage. He had been warned of all sorts of possible eventualities, including a visit to the moors which meant taking a gun and cartridges. He was looking forward to seeing Lord and Lady Sells again and the Grays and meeting May. It was three years since his last visit.

The train journey north was uneventful and he recognised the coachman who had come to meet him. He welcomed him, 'Good afternoon, Sir, Mr David was very sorry he could not be here to meet you but he has had to go out with his father. It is quite some years since you were here, it is nice to see you again.'

'Thank you, Bramwell, I have been looking forward to this visit. I trust all goes well with you?'

'Yes, thank you, Sir, I have been married since you were here and we are now expecting our first child. His Lordship has given us ever such a nice cottage to live in.'

At that he climbed up on the box beside Bramwell where they could continue their conversation. As they journeyed Reg learnt a lot of local news, most of which was of little interest. He did learn however that in a few days' time the Earl hoped to win the gold cup at York.

'Have you heard anything of Mr Gray?' Reg asked.

'No, Sir, but I did hear that his Missus had been very poorly and was in hospital. I have never set eyes on him since I came to pick up you young gentlemen.'

As they approached the Lodge, Bramwell stopped and said, 'Would you mind taking your seat in the carriage, I am not supposed to have anyone on the box with me.' Reg duly complied. On arrival at the Lodge, Reg was shown into the drawing room where he found Lady Sells alone.

'Come on in, Reg, and sit down,' and she beckoned him to a seat on the sofa beside her. 'You have grown even more than David since you were last here. David is out with his father; they should be back soon. There is a big race meeting starting tomorrow and they are both involved in some way. However, this will give me an opportunity to catch up with all your news without interruption.'

They were deep in conversation when the most attractive young lady walked in.

'You remember Caroline, Reg, she like you has grown up since you last met.

Reg jumped up and shook her by the hand. Caroline was of average height, well furnished everywhere as are many girls of her age. She had fair hair worn in ringlets and had the most disarming smile. She sat down and the conversation continued. It was nearly seven by the time David and his father returned. After a short greeting they dispersed to change for dinner. At dinner, at which there were two daughters present, Reg learnt that the next day he and David were to drive themselves to the races and that Caroline would go with them.

On this information becoming known, Lord Sells turned to Reg and said, 'I would be most grateful if you would accompany Caroline for the day.'

'That would be a great pleasure for me,' he replied.

After dinner Caroline came up to him and said, 'Thank you,

Reg, I hope you don't mind but I did wish to get out of the family party, we will have much more fun by ourselves. David tells me that you do quite a lot of driving at home. I think you had better drive tomorrow, David is not much good, he hardly ever drives.'

'You will have to talk to David about that,' Reg replied. Her real motive in making this suggestion was to make it possible for her to sit up with the driver and not in the back by herself.

Next morning was a beautiful summer morning and looked like staying that way. David's party were to make quite an early start as David had to be at the course in good time. He had been recruited to act as assistant paddock steward. When their vehicle arrived at the door David went to take the reins, saying to Reg, 'You come up with me and Caroline can sit in comfort behind.'

'Oh, David,' she said, 'why don't you let Reg drive, you know he is a much better driver than you and I will sit beside him and show him the way.'

It was a good try but David did not give way. David drove perfectly well and when they arrived they found several grooms waiting to take their carriage, feed and water the horse and if requested bring it back at an arranged time. David said he would like it after the last race. David then said, 'I will meet you at the Steward's tent at 12.45. I must go and see about my job.

It was then about noon so Caroline suggested to Reg that they go and see some of the horses. She seemed quite familiar with the place so off they went. As they moved she hung onto his arm pretending to be frightened of the horses. She never stopped talking, questioning him about himself and all the wonderful holidays she had heard about from David. 'We never go anywhere.' In this she was right; she had been educated with a governess and apart from visits to her grandfather and the odd visit to the races that had been her life. About 12.30 they returned to the centre of things and they began to meet a few people she had met here on previous occasions. She took great pride in introducing Reg. As planned, they met David and also her parents. Lunch in the Steward's tent was a very social affair and she was really enjoying herself. This was the first time she had been free from either mother's hand or that of her governess. Reg, too was enjoying himself, it was interesting meeting many new people. Most of the conversation was about the races but Caroline was amazed how easily Reg conversed on any subject.

As the time of the big race approached they found their way to the paddock to see her grandfather's horse which was one of the favourites. During the race she got so excited, she hung onto Reg's arm and jumped up and down. Grandfather's horse did win which was of course the highlight of the day. Eventually it was time to go home. As they went to mount their carriage David said, 'You drive home, Reg, and I will sit in the back.' The return journey was quite uneventful.

That evening Caroline said to her mother, 'Mother, I had a lovely time with Reg, he is such a clever boy. He always seemed to know about everything anyone talked about and sometimes he was very funny.'

Reg wrote in his journal, 'I spent the day at the races looking after Caroline. She is a charming girl but has little conversation, but asks plenty of questions. I enjoyed the day and met many interesting people. They included . . .' and he listed as many as he could remember.

That evening Reg learnt that he, David and the two elder girls had been invited by David's grandparents to a family lunch party the day after next. Next morning David took him round the stud.

He really enjoyed looking at these magnificent animals. He wished his father had a stud, what a wonderful hobby this must be. The afternoon was spent helping to entertain the younger members of the family in the garden. It gave him great pleasure playing with the young, something he was not used to. Next morning the four young people drove over to the lunch party. Reg was welcomed by the Earl and Countess, both of whom remembered him from his previous visit. There were some twelve young people between the ages of fifteen and eighteen plus one or two parents. It was a jolly afternoon but provided little worthy of inclusion in the journal. That evening Reg enquired of David if he had seen anything of the Grays recently.

'No, I don't think I have seen them since you were here.'

Reg stated that he would like to see them again as he had enjoyed their last visit so much. They eventually decided that Reg would write them a letter asking if it would be convenient if they paid them a visit in ten days' time after their return from the moors.

On Sunday they attended the usual family church parade. On Monday morning Lord Sells and the two boys left for the moors. This time they were to sleep in the main house as they formed part of the shooting party. However, they arrived up in time for the two boys to pay a call on Mr and Mrs Williams. They were delighted to see them and they had difficulty getting away in time for dinner. The report from the keeper was that grouse were scarce this year so the Earl was not coming up and Lord Sells restricted the party to five guns which included the two boys. The other two were to be Jack Green, his brother-in-law and Tom Millar, a neighbour. By the time the boys got back Jack had arrived, Tom was just coming by the day.

The morning, when they awoke, was dull and almost looked

as if it might rain. 'Well,' said David, 'it will be a lot cooler walking than it would have been if the hot weather had continued.' At breakfast Lord Sells told the boys that they were to be on the two flanks and they were given very strict instructions on safety. Fortunately, it did not rain and by lunchtime the bag was eight brace and each boy had opened his account. They saw a few more birds in the afternoon and the final bag was twenty and a half brace. After a very pleasant evening during which Jack, who had been a pretty wild young man, kept them amused with his stories, they retired to bed.

The next day was hotter and as there were even fewer birds they covered more ground. They finished with eighteen brace. Both boys had shot well and contributed their share of the bag. The next day they returned to the Lodge.

Next morning the postman brought a letter for Reg from Mr Gray. He said he would be delighted to see the boys next week and that it would be quite in order whatever day they arrived. David consulted his parents and it was agreed that they would drive themselves up on Monday next. In two days, it was Sunday again and they attended the family church parade as before. As they emerged from the church the Earl, who attended the same church, called to David and said, 'Didn't you say that your friend Reg had won a scholarship for Cambridge, bring him back to lunch with us, I would like to talk to him,' and so the two boys returned with the Earl for lunch. The house party had dispersed and there were only four at table. They had a long and animated conversation which continued sitting out in the garden. The Earl enjoyed talking to such a bright young man who was so well informed on so many subjects. He was particularly interested to hear of Reg's trips to St Andrews and about his stalking and fishing holiday.

'What are you going to do when you have finished your studies?'

'I am undecided but I was considering joining the Indian Civil Service.'

When they finally took their leave the Earl said to Reg, 'You must come again, I like talking with you.'

'Thank you very much, Sir,' and they were driven away.

On the way home David said to Reg, 'You got on very well with the old man, it is ages since I saw him in such good form.'

They set off next morning for their visit to the Grays. They followed the same procedure as before and lunched and rested their horse at the same inn. When they drew up at the front door it was opened almost immediately and out came Caroline and June.

'We saw the carriage from Mother's window and thought it might be you. June, run and find someone to take the horse,' Caroline said and then continued, 'Father was expecting you. Unfortunately, Mother is unwell and is upstairs. She is planning to come down for a little this evening, she is anxious to meet you again.'

Caroline had grown into a tall, rather plain girl not unlike her mother.

'How are your father and May?' the boys asked.

'They are both well, they have gone into the village but will be back soon. May does the housekeeping now since our mother's illness.'

'Are you sure we will not be too much of a burden?' David asked.

'Oh, no, everything goes on as normal and we have an extra maid.'

At that moment June returned with the groom and the tablemaid came through the door. The groom was the same man as before and they shook hands. Caroline conducted them into the sitting room where Reg said to her, 'You have grown a lot since we were last here.'

Blushing slightly, she replied, 'I don't think I am the only one to have grown.'

'Oh no,' said Reg, 'I suppose we all have.'

The boys declined the offer of afternoon tea and they sat and talked. They learnt that poor Mrs Gray had been in hospital and they understood that her trouble was tuberculosis.

Suddenly the door burst open and in ran May. She had not grown much taller but had obviously matured considerably. She rushed up to the boys saying, 'Welcome back, we often talked about you and wondered if we would ever see you again.' Turning to Reg, 'Your letter to Father came as a wonderful surprise.'

In minutes Mr Gray walked in and there was another round of greetings. They soon dispersed to find their rooms and change for dinner. When Mr and Mrs Gray entered the room before dinner, what a shock the boys got. Their hostess was just a shadow of her former self and leaned heavily on her husband's arm. She shook hands with both boys and then, turning to Reg, said, 'We were so pleased to receive your kind letter and to learn that you wished to pay us another visit.' She ate very little dinner and obviously had difficulty breathing. Mr Gray however was his usual cheerful self and they had a very happy reunion party. Next morning at breakfast May played the part of hostess and Reg thought what an attractive young lady she had become. She was shorter than her younger sister but was brimming over with vitality.

After breakfast Mr Gray took the boys down to the mill with him. On the way he explained that he would introduce them to a young man called Bill Severn. 'This place is growing too fast for me and having no son I have engaged Bill to help me. He is a farmer's son who trained as an engineer,' and with a wink he added, 'I think he has his eye on May.' Bill was a huge jovial young man with slightly curly red hair. Mr Gray explained that he was planning to build a new granary, to add six additional millstones and a new warehouse for the finished flour. All this was to be built along the railway siding for easy access. Bill showed them the plans and then took them out and showed them on the ground. David did not show too much interest but Reg was fascinated and asked many questions. That afternoon the girls took the boys for a walk round the farm. Mrs Gray did not come down for dinner that evening. Before retiring the boys announced that they would be returning home next day.

Next morning, having taken their leave, Reg took the reins. On seeing this Mr Gray called out, 'Be careful he does not chuck you out, David.'

'I will,' he shouted back as they drove off.

That night at dinner Reg explained to his host all the plans Mr Gray had for expanding his mill.

'He really is a very enterprising man, I must ask him along to shoot again some day,' his host commented.

Reg, thinking that he knew Caroline well enough, started teasing her. She was not used to this and protested while really enjoying the attention.

'I was about to invite you to come and stay with us sometime but now I am wondering if such an invitation would be acceptable.'

'I would love to do that but how would I make the journey?'

'I will write to you, if I may, but it will not be for some time as I am about to start my first term at Cambridge.'

Reg left next morning for home. He stopped off for one night, as usual, with Peter. Peter too had left school and was about to start in his father's office. Back home again Reg reported to his family on his holiday and started to prepare for Cambridge.

Chapter 5

When Reg had been in Cambridge for his exam he learnt what would be required to set himself up should he be successful. Freshmen were requested to arrive several days before term to give themselves time to get settled in. Reg, as a scholar, was allotted a room in college. His apartment, as it were, consisted of a study, a bedroom and a pantry all within an outer door. His rooms were on the second floor and looked out over a courtyard. His bedroom, the window of which was fitted with iron bars to prevent anyone climbing in, faced a narrow street. During those first few days he learnt a lot from his gyp as the result of which he went shopping, something he was not accustomed to. One essential he did acquire was a gown which he was required to wear to lectures and if out after dark. He met his tutor and discovered where his lectures were held. As he was studying agriculture and forestry some of these were quite far out so he decided to buy a bicycle.

He soon began to get into the routines of university life, in some ways it was like a relaxed form of school. As he had never been very keen on team sport he tended to mix more with the country gentleman type, those keen on hunting and shooting. Amongst these there was a certain Jack Y. It was quite some time before Reg discovered his real name. Y was a stoutish fair haired young man, quite clever, who enjoyed life to the full. He was reading law and hoped one day to be either a QC or a politician. Naturally, he had joined the Union and he persuaded Reg to join too. These two young men, although very different in character, became close friends. Reg had the brains and the knowledge while Y was an extrovert, full of confidence, who was popular in every society. They did not meet every day but would fetch up in one of their rooms after dinner once or twice a week. They started inviting others to join them and slowly the group grew.

By the time term ended Reg had settled into university life very easily. He was a natural academic, he liked the easy-going social life and with his bicycle he had explored the immediate neighbourhood of Cambridge.

On arriving home for the Christmas vacation he found Mary far from well. She had lost weight and looked very frail. Because of her condition no social activities were planned for the festive season except for the New Year shoot. His father gave him the letters he had received from Arthur to read. Arthur, who had never been looked on as a good correspondent, had excelled himself and Reg found his letters most interesting about both the progress of the war and the nature of the country.

It was soon apparent to Reg that he was going to be fully occupied. His father wished him to organise the shoot and he wished to get in as many days hunting as possible. In addition he had an invitation from Felicity for two days hunting with them. Slowly he began to realise that horses were becoming of ever-increasing interest, first from the hunting point of view, but those visits in the summer where he saw all those beautiful brood mares attracted him. These thoughts had been passing through his head as he ate his breakfast. Suddenly, he was brought down to earth by his father's voice.

'Reg, will you deal with the invitations for the shoot for me. I find writing very difficult now.'

After preparing the invitation list he persuaded his father to write to one or two of his oldest friends and agreed that he would write to the rest. In addition, he knew that he should write to Uncle Robert on his first term at Cambridge. All this letter writing he did in the evening, leaving him time to plan his hunting programme with the head groom and the shoot with the head keeper.

After a couple of days out with hounds he decided that his father's hunters were more suited both in age and temperament to an elderly gentleman than to a young fellow like him. When he caught up with Ken Oliver a day or two later he asked him to look out for something more suitable. Ken, although not a great horseman himself, was a shrewd man and his judgement could be relied on.

'Very good, Mr Reg, but what are you prepared to pay?' Ken asked. This was a question Reg had not been asked before. After some discussion they agreed that they would both make some enquiries and then meet again. That evening Reg raised the subject with his father and suggested that Christmas was just on them. His father had always been generous to him which made him hesitant to ask for favours. His suggestion was not taken up and Reg thought, well that's that.

Christmas was a very quiet affair with Mary not well and his mother beginning to enjoy the role of grandmother. Reg invited Ken Oliver to shoot on the first day and he, his wife Olive and the twins for dinner that night. The first day proved to be an almost perfect shooting day with a touch of frost and no wind. The result was a good bag and a day which everyone enjoyed. That evening Reg really was amazed at what a good looking pair of girls Ann and Isobel Oliver had become. He had not seen them together for over a year. They were still incredibly alike and went out of their way to make it so. He was not attracted to them as he was to Felicity; they were just like two very amusing sisters to him. The three of them had a lot of fun pulling the legs of some of the more susceptible elderly gentlemen present. The next day's shoot was abandoned owing to snow. Reg hoped it was not going to continue and upset his visit to the Darts.

He was fortunate, as when he awoke on Thursday morning the snow had turned to rain and the ground was bare. He was to be mounted by his hosts so he only had to get himself there. Although he was returning on Monday it was surprising how much luggage he required: one case for his hunting kit plus a hat box and a second large case with his tail coat for Friday night, a dinner jacket for Saturday night, and a tidy suit for Sunday and all the appropriate shoes.

It was getting dark when he alighted from the train. He was delighted to see waiting for him the same young cabbie that he had found the last time. This time he had been warned that he would find a familiar young man on the train. He welcomed Reg with a cheery, 'Good evening, Sir, it is nice to see you back again. It won't be cricket this time, down for a few days with the hounds, are you?'

'Yes indeed, I am a fortunate young man,' Reg replied.

As the cab drew up at the front steps the footman came out with an umbrella which he held over the young guest while he settled his fare. He received a great welcome from all the family, especially the younger members. He was always a great favourite with young children.

He was the only guest at the dinner table that night and conversation flowed freely as it did for the rest of the evening.

His host and hostess were particularly interested to hear about his holiday with David and his first term at Cambridge. He in his turn had much to learn from Felicity, after all it was five months since they had met, although it was true that a few letters had passed between them. Before retiring he was told the time of breakfast and that they would be hacking on next morning leaving at ten fifteen.

When he came down next morning it was light enough to see that the rain had stopped and there was every prospect of it being a good hunting day. There was, building up inside him, quite a degree of excitement. He was to be mounted on a strange horse and one provided by a family who had a reputation for high spirited horses and who were renowned cross-country riders. After a hearty breakfast he presented himself immaculately but soberly dressed in a black coat soon after ten o'clock. Almost immediately he was joined by the family. The two ladies wore dark blue habits, hats and veils, while Sir Richard cut a very dashing figure in a swallowtail which on account of its slightly faded colour must have seen many seasons. Through the window Reg saw four horses led up, each with a rug over its back. 'Reg,' he heard Felicity say, 'you're to ride Red Rupert, he is a great horse, he will be six this spring. We hunted him quite a bit last season and he has been going brilliantly this season.'

'Thank you,' he replied, 'aren't you taking a risk putting a novice like me on such a good horse?'

'Oh no!' she said, 'I am sure you are a super horseman.'

As they emerged from the front door the grooms whipped off the rugs and tightened up the girths. The ladies who were riding side-saddle mounted from a block and Sir Richard walked over to a bay horse which left a beautiful well bred chestnut for Reg. In no time they were all mounted and ready to move off. Sir

Richard and Lady Dart led the way down the drive followed by Reg and Felicity. Red Rupert was very much on his toes and treated Reg to a few little bucks.

'He will soon settle down,' Felicity said. 'Young horses are often like that with a cold saddle.'

After about twenty minutes they came to the meeting place outside a small inn. Felicity introduced Reg to several other followers before hounds moved off to the first draw. This proved blank and hounds were taken at a smart canter to the next covert. This gave Reg an opportunity to feel the power and smoothness of his thoroughbred mount.

'Gone Away' they heard and in no time they heard the hounds cry. Red Rupert cocked his ears and lifted his head. He knew what that cry meant. The Master held up the field to give the pack time to settle to the line. Once released there was a bit of a charge to the first fence, a beautifully cut and laid hedge of fair proportions. Reg made sure that Red Rupert had every opportunity to see the fence and they sailed over in great style. It was not long before the front ranks began to thin out. Some fell, some refused and the bulk simply could not match the pace. After about fifteen minutes, hounds checked and everyone had time to draw breath. A quick look round told Reg that not only Felicity but her parents were there. Felicity began to move towards Reg, who had been riding a little to one side to ensure he did not interfere with hounds or obstruct the regular followers.

'How do you like him?' she asked.

'Absolutely perfect,' he replied.

Then they were off again and they were riding side by side. The horses, being stablemates, were obviously enjoying being together. The pace was not so hot and Reg loved watching hounds puzzle out the line. Suddenly the pace quickened. What a thrill it was to ride such a brilliant horse. Reg did not realise it at the time but this experience was going to have a lasting influence on his life. They hunted on for some thirty minutes with some fast bursts interspersed with the occasional check. They finally bowled over their fox just short of a thick gorse covert. Felicity suggested that they should hack home and keep their horses for tomorrow. She explained that they did not often hunt two days running but that today had been a special New Year Meet. They slackened their girths and as they passed told her parents, who both had a second horse in the stable for the next day.

As they rode home Reg kept repeating how much he had enjoyed Red Rupert. He told Felicity that he had already asked Ken Oliver to start looking for a horse for him.

'I think you should talk to Papa, he has a rather nice half-brother to Red Rupert who is just four which he might be prepared to part with. You ask him if you can see him and if you like him I will put a word in for you.'

They were home in a little over thirty minutes. The footman served them with a quick cup of tea and a piece of cake before they went for a bath and change. Having bathed, Reg, armed with his journal, thought that he might slip into the library and there write it up while the day was still fresh in his mind. As he passed the study door his host emerged and enquired where he was going. Having disclosed his intention Sir Richard said, 'Come along in here,' and he retired to his study. Once inside Sir Richard continued, 'Enjoyed your day? I thought you rode that young horse very well.'

'Thank you, Sir, he was so easy to ride and taught me the difference between a really good horse and one of the old plodders we have in the stable at home. I was telling Felicity that I had already started looking for a younger horse and she suggested that you might have something which might suit me. She mentioned a half brother to Red Rupert.'

'She has been trying to sell you one of my best up and coming hunters has she?' and he laughed. 'I tell you what, you can start on him tomorrow and after half an hour or so change to Red Rupert.'

Reg's breath was almost taken away, 'Do you mean that?' he stammered.

'Of course I mean it, that's the plan for tomorrow. Now you write up your journal here while I go and have a good soak in the bath.'

Reg sat there looking at his journal, wondering what had prompted him to suggest to Sir Richard that he could be interested in buying a young horse from him. He knew that first he could not afford to do so, and second that even if he could it would be a waste of money while he was still a student. However, he was looking forward to tomorrow. Having sorted things out in his mind he applied himself to his journal until it was time to change for dinner. They were to be dining at home and then going out to the dance in a neighbour's house about three miles away. Reg did not disclose at dinner that he had already decided that he could not buy the young horse, as he was longing to have a ride on him tomorrow.

The dance proved to be a fairly small affair, probably less than fifty in total. Nevertheless he met a lot of interesting people. His host and hostess were elderly and were giving the party for their grand-daughter who was very much Felicity's age. Having learnt this, Reg felt it was his duty to offer to dance with her. Although she was a decorative little thing Reg was not attracted to her, feeling that she was probably all just fluff. As he approached her he hoped her programme would be full but no, she would be delighted to dance with him. When, some time later, he went to claim his dance he found his partner remonstrating with a young man who was claiming her hand. For a moment he thought this might be a let-out but as soon as she saw him she left the other man and joined him.

'Thank goodness you have rescued me from that man,' she said, 'I wanted to dance with you, not with him.'

They took to the floor and nothing more was said. She danced beautifully, very close to him. As the music stopped she took him by the hand and led him from the floor.

'Let's go and sit out.' They found a quiet corner and sat down. Up till then hardly a word had passed between them but suddenly she started, 'I saw you leading the field on that super horse of the Darts'. What do you think of him? I would like to buy him as a chaser.' There followed a long discussion about horses, after which she started quizzing him about himself. When the music started again, rather reluctantly, she said, 'We must go, I do hope we can meet again.' Before seeking out his next partner he recorded her name and address inside his programme. Felicity had warned Reg not to book the last two dances as her parents wished to go home at that point and as they were all travelling in the same carriage they must leave then too. Reg had very much enjoyed the evening which had included a dance with Lady Dart.

At breakfast next morning Sir Richard warned him not to expect too much of the young horse and to keep him well clear of hounds. 'After about half an hour swap onto Red Rupert and enjoy the rest of your day.'

Lady Dart and Felicity drove to the meet so Reg hacked on with Sir Richard. Red Wolf was another well bred but bay horse this time. At the meet Reg kept well out of harm's way and, when mounted, Felicity came over and joined him.

It was quite some time before the first fox was found. The pace was slow compared to yesterday, which suited Reg and he took the opportunity to pop over a couple of small fences. When they were waiting at the next check the groom arrived with Red Rupert and Reg swapped horses. Unfortunately, the day turned out to be one of those exasperating days with few foxes and very little scent. However, it did give an opportunity for conversation and several people congratulated Reg on his mount. He had to explain that he was not his.

That evening they were joined for dinner by a Mr and Mrs Risk and their son and daughter. After dinner they played cards before retiring quite early. Next morning, over a leisurely breakfast, Sir Richard asked Reg how he had got on with Red Wolf.

'Oh, I enjoyed my ride on him very much; he is going to make a super hunter.'

'Do you still want to buy him?' he asked.

'I would love to,' replied Reg, 'if I had the money and what is more to the point if I had the time to ride him. I know that I would be foolish to buy a good young horse just to stand and eat his head off at home until I have finished at Cambridge.'

Sir Richard agreed and the subject was dropped. After Church and lunch a visit to the stables was the order of the day. The more Reg saw of these beautiful thoroughbred horses the more he felt himself getting drawn towards them. That evening he had long discussions with Sir Richard about horse breeding and farming. Next morning his faithful cabbie arrived to take him to the station. He could not imagine a happier weekend.

Back home again he only had a few days before he had to return to his studies. However, he did have time for lunch with the Olivers where the girls were both still at home. He spent much of lunch discussing horses with Ken and extolling the virtues of Red Rupert. They decided not to look for a young horse but for one a little less staid than those in the stable. After lunch he had a happy afternoon with the twins.

Back at Cambridge he, egged on by Y, made his first speech at the Union. It was not as frightening as he expected.

He started following up some advertisements for horses for sale and he and Y had gone to have a look at a couple. He liked having Y with him as he was a much more experienced bargainer than he was. So far the animals inspected had fallen so far short of what he was looking for that they had not got involved in serious bargaining. Then one day he received a letter from Ken saying he had located a possible horse and was arranging to have it on trial during the Easter vacation. It was due to arrive the day after his return. He told his parents of his plans. Next evening, when he received a message from the stables that the horse had arrived he rushed up to have a look at him. He was indeed a fine looking bay horse about 16 hands 1 inch. He made immediate plans to try him next morning. Ken met him at the stables next morning and told him all he had heard about the horse which included the warning that he was inclined to take a hold and that some people had a problem stopping him. As he had been in a racing stable he had only been ridden in a snaffle bit and might resent something stronger. Reg decided to risk the snaffle and set off accompanied by one of the grooms riding one of his father's old hunters. They walked and trotted along the road and all went fine and Reg was becoming more and more delighted, he seemed a nice horse.

On the way home they turned into the big field in which were the schooling fences. Reg asked the groom to watch while he gave the Baron, as that was his name, a canter round. Everything went well, he felt super at the canter so Reg allowed him to push on a bit and still he came to hand quite easily. Returning to the groom he asked him to accompany him over one of the schooling fences. They cantered up the field together but as soon as the Baron saw the fence in front of him he took hold of the bit and off he charged. He flew over the fence in great style and on he went. They were galloping slightly uphill and Reg hoped he would be able to stop him by confronting him with the large hedge at the top. He was wrong; as soon as he saw the hedge he quickened and nothing Reg tried made any difference. Before he knew where he was he was at the fence and over they went. On the other side there was a wide lane and beyond another large fence to the next field. There was quite a drop into the lane which caused the Baron to peck slightly which in turn threw Reg forward in the saddle. 'I hope I can stick on if he jumps this next hedge,' thought Reg; there was just room for one good stride and he would know. Before Reg realised what was happening he found himself flying through the air. The Baron had stuck his toes in and dropping his head and shoulder threw his jockey over the hedge. Reg landed on his back with sufficient force to knock the wind out of him. However, after a few seconds he sat up and realising that there was nothing wrong with him he got to his feet.

He looked over the hedge and there was the Baron standing apparently quite undisturbed. Reg started searching for a place where he could climb back over. By the time he had managed this the groom came riding up the lane. He was thankful to find the young gentleman on his feet. Reg, who was already beginning to feel the effects of his fall, found climbing back into the saddle a little more difficult than he expected. In spite of his fall Reg liked the horse and he felt sure that they could overcome this problem so he decided to ask Ken to make an offer for him. The offer was accepted and the Baron took up residence. Reg was determined to do as much of this re-education himself as possible during the short Easter break. He rode every day and had the Baron well accustomed to a double bridle by the end of the holidays. He was sorry to have to hand over the finishing of this task to the staff although they were competent horsemen. Before the end of the holidays he wrote a letter to Felicity telling her all about the Baron.

Back in Cambridge life was becoming more interesting. With the better weather it was possible to spend more time visiting farms where experimental work was in progress and to talk with those who had actually carried out the research. He continued to attend debates in the Union as a result of which he became aware of his very limited knowledge, particularly on political subjects and public affairs generally. He started reading the newspapers and other publications and slowly he began to wonder where all this was leading him. Up to now life had been technical studies and amusement but he was becoming aware that he could not go through life like that. What did he want to do, that was the problem. Ever since he had met those two ladies on the train he had a desire to learn more about India, there was something about the place which fascinated him. He began to toy with the idea of applying for a job in the Indian Civil Service.

Then one day he received a letter with a black rim round the edge of the envelope. He feared the worst as it was his father's handwriting. On opening it he found a letter from his father telling him of the death of his sister Mary, she had died of TB. He made immediate arrangements to return home as the funeral was to be held in two days' time. Poor Mary, he was going to miss her. Other than his father she had been the one member of the family with whom he had a close relationship. He arrived home the day before the funeral as did his elder sister and her husband, who had not brought their baby son with them.

Next morning the hearse arrived at 10.15 drawn by two black horses. The coffin was carried down and the funeral procession was formed up. It was led by his father behind whom walked Reg and his brother-in-law; Arthur was still in South Africa. Behind them came other relatives, such as the Plumbs. Behind them walked local friends and finally the estate workers. There were no ladies on foot. Reg's mother, accompanied by Olga, led the carriage procession which followed those on foot. It took forty-five minutes to reach the Church. After the service and the internment all friends were invited back for lunch. There were very few ladies but his mother was delighted that her sister, Aunt May, had come.

Next day he returned to Cambridge wearing his black tie which he would probably wear until next holidays. Mary's death and funeral made quite an impression on Reg. He found it difficult to believe he would never see her again. Some days after his return he was in the bookshop when someone touched him on the shoulder. He thought he recognised the voice which addressed him. On turning round, indeed it was Uncle Sam Wilson. Uncle Sam asked him what he was doing for lunch, to which Reg replied that he had no plans.

'Well,' said Uncle Sam, 'you will lunch with me and we will catch up with one another's news. I won't be a minute, I just want to buy some pen nibs. I like a J nib; I expect you like a relief. I will meet you at the door in a few minutes.' As they left the shop Uncle Sam said, 'I know this town well, I don't live very far away. I am going to take you to a small house who serve a good meal. You have grown a lot since last we met, is this your first year?'

'Yes Sir, I am just about to sit my first year exams.'

'What are you reading?'

'Agriculture and Forestry,' Reg replied.

'That is a surprise, I expected you would have been reading law, or history or something like that. What gave you that idea?'

Reg went on to explain all about Uncle Robert and that it was after discussing it with him that he had decided. They turned into a small door which led into a small eating house attached to a public house.

Once they were seated at the table Sam asked, 'Why the black tie? I hope it was not a close relative.'

Reg explained that it was his sister Mary and that she had been ill for some time with TB.

'Oh, I am sorry, I am sure you will miss her. A funny thing life, how some of us survive and others are taken.'

They talked on till suddenly Sam said, 'Would you care to come and spend a Saturday night with me? Your tutor would permit that, wouldn't he?'

'I should like that very much,' whereupon Sam produced a card with his name and address and explained how to find him. Reg explained that he had a bicycle but that was a little difficult for luggage. 'Just bring a small bag, we will not bother to change on Saturday night – you can do these things when you are a bachelor.' They fixed a date which Reg promised to confirm by letter. Lunch finished they each went their own way.

My readers must remember that in Reg's day the Universities received no financial assistance from the state; they were financially independent raising revenue from students' fees, services provided and from rents. Many of the colleges were quite large landowners. Most students' fees were being paid by their parents and because of this colleges took a more parental interest in their students than today. Reg had no difficulty obtaining permission and quickly confirmed his acceptance of the invitation.

Late in the afternoon some twelve days later Reg set off to ride the ten miles to Little Bewell with his case strapped firmly on the carrier of his bicycle. He did not hurry, he enjoyed looking at the countryside as he peddled along. He had no difficulty finding the house as Uncle Sam had given him very clear directions. The two-story medium sized house was set in beautifully kept grounds. The door was opened by a tall grey haired domestic.

'Come along in, Sir, Mr Wilson told me to expect you.' She took the case from the bicycle and closed the door. 'I will just show you the downstairs before I take you to your room.'

On the left of the hall was the drawing room, beautifully furnished, very tidy and it did not look as if it was much used. Across the hall was the dining room, comparable in size, with rather heavy Victorian furniture. As they crossed back across the hall she said, 'Mr Wilson is just out for a walk with his dog, I am sure he won't be long.' Behind the drawing room was the study. This was quite a large room with a bow window looking out to the garden, on one side of which was a door into the garden. The room was comfortably furnished with a large writing desk in one corner. There was a bookcase and papers and books everywhere.

'Mr Wilson does not like us to tidy this room, he cannot find anything if we do.'

'Thank you,' said Reg.

'Oh, you are welcome, Sir.'

'Has Mr Wilson lived here long?' asked Reg.

'It must be getting on for fifteen years. When he bought it he spent a lot of money modernising it. He renewed the plumbing, installed central heating, and electric light.'

'Have you been here all that time?' enquired Reg.

'Oh yes, and for some time before, I was sort of bought with the place, as you might say.'

'How very interesting, you will have many tales to tell about this house.'

'Oh no, Sir, it wouldn't be proper for me to tell tales.'

Reg was just hoping to learn a little more when he heard footsteps in the hall. Mr Wilson, having left his dog in the kennel, had come in by the back door.

'Well, Reg, you have got here all right, is Mary showing you all my secrets?'

'What a delightful room this is,' replied Reg.

'Mary, show the young man his room and after you have sorted yourself out we will have time for a quick look at the garden and a drink before dinner.'

Reg's room was right above the study and it only took him minutes before he was down again. He found Uncle Sam reading the newspaper. When he heard Reg he put it down and said, 'Come along, I wish to take you for a short walk round outside just to show you the set-up before we have a drink.'

They went out through the study door and as they strolled along Reg said what a delightful person Mary was. 'Reg,' Uncle Sam replied, 'I could not be more fortunate. I have her and a gardener called Dick whose wife Ann cooks for me. They have their house in the garden and then I have a young single groom who lives above the stable. He has not enough to do with just one horse so he helps in the garden.'

About fifty yards behind the house they came to the kitchen garden. It was walled on two sides and in the far corner was Dick's house. Just outside the garden was the stable block with stabling for four horses and two carriages. As they looked into the coach house there was Reg's bicycle. It had been brought round by Jim the groom. And so they returned to the study for a drink.

Uncle Sam was keen to learn what Reg had been doing since they last met, which was after all some eighteen months ago. Reg started by telling of his sister Mary's death.

'You will miss her, she was the one you used to mention when last we met.'

'Yes, my elder sister is married and Arthur, as you know, is away in the army and at present in South Africa.' This led to a discussion about the Boer War after which they moved through for dinner. They were very well looked after by Mary. Reg described the wonderful few days he had with Felicity and her parents, not forgetting the horses and, of course, he had to mention the Baron.

'Have you never been interested in horses?'

'No, not really, I lost too much money on them as a young man so I cut out the betting all together. Don't get involved in the betting, there is more misery caused by that than anything.'

'I have never been interested in betting but I would love to be involved in breeding, they are such beautiful creatures.'

'Have you ever been to a big yard?' asked Uncle Sam.

'Quite a big one,' and Reg described Lord Sells' stable at the Lodge.

'Well,' said Uncle Sam, 'we will get Jim to drive us up to Newmarket tomorrow where I know old Bob Smith, who manages Lord Yobb's establishment. If he is too busy to show us round I am sure he will have someone who can.'

That fixed they moved through to the study where Reg learnt a lot about the management of the countryside from Uncle Sam who was now not only a member of the County Council but also on other local committees.

Next morning, after a good breakfast, they left at nine expecting to cover the ten miles in about an hour and a quarter. They followed side-roads at first and they enjoyed over the fence farming. It was almost ten thirty when they drew up outside a house. They dismounted and rang the bell. The door was opened by a girl who informed them that Mr Smith was in the yard but Mrs Smith was at home. They were shown into a sitting room when almost immediately Mrs Smith swept into the room. She was a well covered woman with a reddish face and a very welcoming manner.

'Well, Sam, it is nice to see you, you are a stranger. What brings you here?' Sam introduced Reg and explained his interest in horses. They shook hands. She did not let go of his hand but led him to the back door and out into the yard. They walked together over to a small group of men.

'Dad, this young man has just walked in with Sam Wilson; he wants to see the horses. I am going back to talk to Sam.'

After a few more words Mr Smith dismissed the lads and turned and took Reg by the hand. 'So you are a friend of Sam, a great gentleman is Sam. What can I do for you?'

Reg explained that he was a student at Cambridge and was spending the weekend with Mr Wilson.

'Are you a relative of Sam's?'

'No,' and Reg explained in some detail how he and Sam had first met and their chance meeting in Cambridge some ten days earlier. 'Last night we were chatting and I happened to mention my growing attraction towards thoroughbred horses and his immediate action was to bring me up here today.'

'That is enough for me; any friend of Sam is a friend of mine until we fall out,' and he laughed. 'Come on, let's go and see the second string come in from work.'

They walked through a passage which led them into a second yard of boxes. They walked to the centre where they stood talking for a few minutes before the first of the string entered the yard.

They formed a circle round Bob and their riders dismounted. Bob then walked up to the leader, asked the rider for his report and then dismissed him to his box. He followed this with a visit to each box where he had a brief word with the lad. Once that was over it was time to return to his house.

As they entered the sitting room Mrs Smith said, 'Sam and his young friend will be staying for a bite of lunch with us; now you look after them while I pop through to the kitchen.' In minutes she was back with a tray of glasses and they all partook of a toast to this reunion. Lunch was a very jolly affair with much reminiscing after which Uncle Sam said he thought it was time to take their leave. As they said good-bye, Bob said to Reg, 'Would you be interested to come and spend a few days with us and see how the place functions?'

'Yes indeed,' Reg replied, 'but it would have to be in the vacation which starts in four weeks' time. If I may, I will check with my parents to ensure that they have not made any commitments for me and then I will write to you.'

On the way home Reg learnt that not only were the Smiths very good company but that Bob was considered one of the best trainers. After dinner Reg learnt all about the development and growth of the Wilson industrial empire. This made Reg think about his future. Although his father had supplied him with a reasonable income he knew that he must eventually find some way to augment it. Next morning he mounted his bicycle and returned to Cambridge.

That evening, having written his letter of thanks to Uncle Sam and one to his father about his proposed visit to Newmarket, he started to write up his journal, but somehow he did not know where to start. His weekend with Uncle Sam and the wide ranging discussions they had had started him thinking about his future. Up till now he had thought vaguely that he might apply for a job in the India Office but had given no thought to the financial side of his life. He sat and gazed at his book with his imagination running wild in all directions. His final entry was quite brief but did include a list of questions. Next morning he returned to his normal routine.

A few days later he received a letter from his father. This informed him that there was no reason for him not to go to Newmarket, pointing out what a fortunate young man he was to have been befriended by Mr Wilson and suggesting that in due time he should be included in the guest list for the New Year shoot. He immediately wrote to Bob Smith saying that he was now in a position to accept his kind invitation to spend a few days with them at the end of term and he suggested a date. It was not long before he had confirmation in a letter saying how much they looked forward to entertaining him. It was now time to get down to work and prepare for the first year exams which were only some weeks ahead. It was not long before the exams were over and he was packing his bags for Newmarket.

Mr and Mrs Smith were unfortunately childless; perhaps that was why they were so welcoming to a young man. It may also have contributed to Bob's success as a trainer; his horses were his life. When Reg rang the bell the door was opened by Mrs Smith. She held out her hand saying, 'Welcome Mr Win-Wantock, we do hope you enjoy your few days with us.'

'I know I shall,' was Reg's reply.

Turning to the maid who was standing behind her, Mrs Smith said, 'Jane, take Mr Win-Wantock's bags upstairs please.'

Once in the sitting room Reg said, 'Mrs Smith, I suggest you call me Reg, Win-Wantock is such a mouthful.'

'Yes, but could I call you Mr Reg, I think I would find that easier. I know Bob will want you to address him as Bob and you can call me Rose.'

Reg replied, 'I will find Bob no problem but may I call you Mrs Smith?'

'Very good, that's all settled.'

They sat and chatted about life as a student and about his home. Mrs Smith was delighted to find what an easy young man he was to talk to. After a short time Mrs Smith said, 'Let's go and see if Bob is in his office. I am sure he would like to know that you have arrived.'

The office was situated just inside the door to the yard and sure enough there he was.

As soon as he saw Reg he jumped up and shaking him warmly by the hand exclaimed, 'Just the man I need, someone who knows how to push a pen. When you have horses from different owners I like to keep some notes in case I get muddled. The one who does the real clerical work is Rose, she looks after all the money matters. Nowadays with the railways you are expected to run horses all over the place. There is a lot of work with transport, stabling and so on. Whenever possible I like to go myself. We have seven horses running on Wednesday and Thursday but fortunately it is here this week. Come on, let's go and see what is going on outside, the lads should be coming back for evening stables.'

At that time the boxes received their last muck out, the horses were watered, fed and the hay racks filled. After that they were shut up for the night. As they crossed the yard they met an elderly man with a barrow, a shovel and a broom.

'Finished for the day, Dick? Dick keeps the yard and in his spare time does a bit of gardening. Dick was a good jockey in his day.'

'Thank you, Sir, I always tried my best, that's all a man can do.'

They walked round and inspected those horses which were to run tomorrow and Bob had a word with each lad as they met. In the stud yard, there were six larger boxes which were used for foaling or for any stallions. At present there was only one stallion which belonged to Bob's main employer. The other boxes were empty, the mares and foals being out to grass. They returned to the house and Bob, who was a very moderate drinker, suggested just one to celebrate Reg's visit. What a wonderful evening he had, picking Bob's brains on everything to do with horses and racing. They retired early as they were to ride work next morning at six thirty.

Next morning, Reg was given a ride on one of the racehorses but of course not one of those to run that day. When he got back at eight he was ready for his breakfast. Bob and Rose ran a very philanthropic establishment for their staff. They had a hostel with mess room for the lads and staff to provide their meals. After breakfast Bob did not ride work but sent Reg out with the head lad. On their return Bob suggested that Reg 'looked to' his horse under the eagle eye of his lad. Reg was delighted, he had so often seen a horse groomed but had never actually done it himself. He was young and the physical work appealed to him and he offered to help whenever an opportunity arose. The next day followed the same pattern, with one difference. This time the horse he rode behaved perfectly outside but proved to be one of those unreliable customers inside. His lad, anxious that no harm became the young gentleman, warned Reg of the problem. Reg learnt some good lessons on how to avoid being bitten in the bottom and much else besides.

The following day was race day and he took special note of the programme of those horses which were to run. As the racecourse was not too far away the horses were able to hack on. The procedure at the course was much the same as he had witnessed at York. Bob had two winners and one 'also ran' out of his three runners, and was pleased with the day's results.

Reg volunteered to ride early exercise next morning and again after breakfast to groom each of the horses concerned. This relieved the pressure on the lads who were getting the four horses ready for the races. That afternoon Bob had two horses running in the third race, the big race of the day. Reg was holding one of them while the lad put the saddle on when he heard, 'I know your face, is that your horse?'

'No, Sir,' Reg replied, 'but I think we did meet some years ago at my father's shoot at Wantock.'

The stranger continued, 'What are you doing here?'

Reg explained that he was staying with Bob Smith, the trainer, and that this was one of his horses.

'What's its name?'

'Bobsleigh,' Reg replied.

'God, that's one of my cousin's horses, I had forgotten he had them with Bob Smith. Is it going to win?'

'I understand he has a very good chance.'

'Thank you and good luck,' and the stranger moved on.

The question was soon answered as Bobsleigh, although the less favoured of Bob's runners, stormed home to win by a head. Later that afternoon Reg was making his way to the paddock when he was stopped by Major Lenn, the gentleman who had spoken to him before the big race.

'Thank you very much for that tip, I had a very good win on Bobsleigh. Would you care to join us for dinner in the hotel to celebrate?' Reg explained that he was short of clothes. 'Never mind that, put on the best you have and come along.'

'Thank you very much, Sir.'

'The name is Major Lenn, and you will meet my cousin Pip, the owner of Bobsleigh, he is joining the party.'

When Reg got home that evening and told Mrs Smith about his invitation, she was quite excited. She ironed his shirt, pressed his trousers and cleaned his shoes. As the hotel was not all that far away Reg decided to walk and Mrs Smith said she would leave the door open and that he could turn the key behind him when he came in.

When Reg arrived at the hotel he was ushered into a private room where there were already five men. It looked like being an all male party and it was obvious that some of them had already started their celebrations. His host introduced him to the other four, usually only using Christian names. All the party appeared to be of his father's vintage and he was much relieved when two younger men appeared, but even they could give him a few years. Drink flowed freely and Reg soon decided that he would have to be very careful. Most of the conversation was confined to the day's racing, to which horses had run well, and to who had made money and who had lost. At dinner he had on his left Adrian, a young man probably in his late twenties, and on his right a venerable white-haired gentleman who everyone addressed as Isy. It was not long before Reg discovered that he was a retired General. The General questioned Reg closely on his background and how he had been invited. Reg found the General very easy to talk to and when he told him that his elder brother was serving in South Africa that opened another door. Adrian, on the other hand, he found very heavy weather. His conversation seemed to be limited to horses or women. The wine certainly loosened up the tongues and as dinner progressed the stories began to get less and less probable. After the port had been round the table several times great was Reg's relief when the General rose and announced that he must be going. This was the signal for everyone to rise from the table and after a short time Reg decided that he could slip away. On the way out he obtained the full name and address of his host from the hall porter.

As Reg walked home he felt a little light headed. He had enjoyed the evening but had found it a bit of a strain, first being so much younger than the others and secondly, trying to avoid drinking too much. Having locked the door he crept upstairs and slipped into bed, hoping that someone would wake him in the morning. Next day was to be his last day and he did not wish to miss any of it. Bob knocked him up at six and although very sleepy he did not feel too bad. The early morning ride out did him a world of good and on his return he was ready for his breakfast. He spent the rest of the morning riding and in the stables.

As they sat eating their lunch Bob turned to Reg and said, 'I am going to tell you something and perhaps it is not my place to do so, but I am like that, I speak my mind.'

Reg could not imagine what was coming.

Bob continued, 'You are the best lad who has ever come into my yard. Not only have you got brains but you co-operated so well in everything. So many young gentlemen are afraid of hard work. I have heard nothing but good from the lads and that is saying something. They usually resent a stranger getting in their way.'

'You embarrass me, Bob,' Reg replied and turning to Mrs Smith said, 'he must think I have a string of horses round the corner somewhere.' Turning back to Bob he continued, 'I could not have enjoyed myself more, everyone has been so kind, when I wished to know something nothing was too much trouble. I found the lads most entertaining. As we were tidying up this morning one of the young ones came up to me and touching his cap said, "Is it true that you are a scholar at Cambridge?" "Yes," I replied, whereupon he exclaimed, "You must be very clever, I have never seen a scholar before." "They are funny looking things aren't they?" They all laughed. "You must be very clever." "No," I said, "I just had the opportunities, you all know much more about horses than I do."'

Bob then said, 'As you are off tomorrow, would you care to spend some time this afternoon discussing how I run this place?'

'If you can spare the time that would be most interesting,' Reg replied.

They talked for a very long time covering everything from brood mares and foals to schooling, training, feeding, health and finally blood lines and breeding.

That evening Reg questioned Bob about the people he had met at the dinner party. Bob filled in quite a lot about some of them, all useful information for Reg's journal. Next morning when Bob was issuing his orders for the day Reg took the opportunity to thank everybody for being so kind to him and said good-bye. When it came to taking his leave of the Smiths there were very warm hand-shakes and an assurance that he would be welcome at any time.

Chapter 6

Reg spent two nights at Cambridge before returning home. He spent most of that day writing up his journal. He visited his tutor to discuss with him his programme for the next year. His tutor informed him that he had heard that those papers corrected so far showed very promising results and he promised to write Reg giving him his full results as soon as they became available.

Back at Wantock he found his parents very subdued. Mary's death had left them on their own for the first time for many years. His father, as always, was anxious to hear all about his activities and for the first time for many years his mother was keen to join in.

'I am longing to hear all about your visit to Newmarket,' she said.

Well Reg, being Reg, had to start at the beginning with his chance meeting with Mr Wilson. This led to his weekend with him and finally to the stay with Bob Smith. Reg covered everything in some detail which took all the first evening. He emphasised how pleased he was to have been encouraged to actually do the work himself and how much more he had learnt as the result. When they got round to discussing his academic studies his mother's interest waned. On one occasion he raised the subject of his future: what was he going to do on coming down from

Cambridge? He told his parents that he was going to explore the possibility of joining the Indian Civil Service. His father thought it a good idea but his mother said, 'Do you wish to go and live out there? We will never see you.' Reg had not confined himself to these discussions, he had been very occupied in other directions. He had enjoyed reading Arthur's letters in one of which he described quite a hot engagement in which he had been involved. They had suffered several casualties but he had returned unscathed.

Reg took long walks round the estate visiting the various employees. On one of these occasions he had come on the Baron out at grass with the other hunters. He visited the Olivers and had long talks with Ken; the twins were away from home. A few days after he got home he received a letter from Ben inviting him to Scotland and suggesting he bring a fishing rod.

He was very attracted by this idea but he felt a little guilty leaving his parents. He raised the question with them and they both told him to go. He wrote to Ben accepting. As he had so often done before, he travelled to London the day before he was to travel to Scotland. He called on the Plumbs hoping to find a bed. Peter was away but his aunt and the others were delighted to see him and there followed a very happy evening exchanging news.

Next morning he arrived at the station in good time and he was glad he was early as being holiday time the platform was crowded and the 3rd Class compartments were very full. However, he found a 1st Class seat without too much difficulty. In the compartment he had selected were a middle aged couple, probably a little younger than his parents. They occupied the two seats at the window. He placed himself in one of the two remaining vacant seats and having placed his rods on the rack he left his hat on his seat and stepped outside. Having stretched his legs for a few minutes he returned to his compartment to find his hat placed on the other seat and a large voluminous woman of uncertain age seated in his seat. She looked up at Reg and, without any apology, said, 'I moved your hat. I cannot sit with my back to the engine. Anyway, where is my maid going to sit with your hat there?'

At that moment a grey haired lady came down the corridor and, popping her head in, said, 'You will be all right there, my Lady,' and turning to Reg said, 'I am so sorry we had to move your hat, I do hope you don't mind.'

Reg wondered for a minute if he should offer to swap seats with the maid but having got all his rods and other gear stowed on the rack he was not keen to do so. The train jerked and started to move, the maid retired and he sat down. Reg occupied himself with his newspaper. After a while, noticing that his lady friend appeared to have nothing to do, he addressed her: 'Excuse me, my Lady, would you care to borrow my newspaper?'

'No,' came a very abrupt reply, 'Mary has my glasses.' She followed this up with, 'And what is your name, young man?'

'My name is Reginald Win-Wantock.' He wanted to say 'and what is yours?' but felt constrained not to do so.

He was just about to return to his paper when she asked, 'Where are you going?'

'Oh, I am going to St Andrews.'

This seemed to satisfy the old lady for there followed a long silence.

Having finished reading his paper Reg folded it up and standing up, placed it on the rack above the old lady and took down a book. Having sat down again he was thumbing through the first few pages when he heard, 'Win-Wantock did you say?'

'Yes,' he replied.

'Was your father known as Colonel Winall?'

'Yes, I think so,' Reg replied.

'He served under my husband, years ago before we went to India.'

'Were you long in India?' Reg asked.

'Yes, my husband died out there two years ago and I had to come home.'

'I am afraid I do not know your name, who was your husband?'

'My husband was General Sir William Basher, everyone knew him in India. Have you ever thought of joining the army?'

'No,' Reg replied, 'but my elder brother is in the army. He is serving in South Africa at the moment. He is due home in six months. May I ask where you are going?'

'I am getting off at Berwick to stay with my daughter in the Borders. Her husband was in the army before he left and returned to look after the family estates. I am quite excited; I shall be there for the 12th. I have never been to a grouse shoot before. Have you?'

'No,' replied Reg but explained that he had been fishing and deer stalking. This opened the door and they had a long conversation, including Newmarket and Cambridge.

Eventually, the waiter announced the first sitting for lunch and Mary arrived to take her Ladyship along. Reg, as he was going through to Edinburgh, had booked the second sitting. When she returned from her lunch she addressed Reg as follows: 'Before you go for your lunch I want to tell you that I have enjoyed meeting you and will you give my kind regards to your father. He probably won't remember me, I was a young bride when last we met and your father unmarried.'

When Reg returned from his lunch the train had passed Berwick and Lady Basher was gone. The rest of the journey was uneventful and Ben met Reg at St Andrews station. Uncle Robert and Aunt

Edith were delighted to see Reg again. He had grown and filled out considerably but was still noticeably smaller than his cousin. What an evening they had. Reg was questioned from all sides and winningly replied. Before they finally went to bed Ben disclosed the plan for the rest of Reg's stay. Next day, being Sunday, they would go to the Kirk in the morning then after lunch take a walk on the links. In the evening they had some friends coming in for supper. Mary and her young brother were both away from home. During the course of Sunday, Reg learnt that on Monday he and Ben would leave by train for the north on a fishing holiday. Their schedule was quite complex: St Andrews, Leuchars, Dundee, Perth, Inverness to Inverpip on the Thurso line. They left early and the journey went well and many interesting contacts were made, but we have not time to interview them here.

At Inverpip station they were met by Uncle Ben, Uncle Robert's brother, after whom our Ben had been named. Uncle Ben's children had all grown up and left home, Uncle Ben being several years older than Uncle Robert. He owned and operated the general store in Inverpip and he and his wife lived in a very nice house above it. The store served a very large area with a very wide variety of products, and if they did not have what you wanted they would get it for you. Uncle Ben, amongst his wide interests, was a keen fisherman and of course sold fishing tackle.

He was a friend to a huge circle of all classes over a large area. Uncle Ben had arranged for the two boys to stay with a shepherd friend in a remote cottage in the hills, Jock Bain and his wife; they had no children and took in a few fishers, their cottage being within easy walking distance of several good trout lochs. Transport was the only problem, the only means of getting there, unless you had private transport, was with the postman. He only visited the Bains on one day a week and that was Wednesday. However,

Uncle Ben had it all arranged. The boys would stay with him for Tuesday and travel on Wednesday; this would give time for the boys to see his old widowed sister who was very keen to see them. They learnt all this as they walked the half mile from the station. Uncle Ben had a regular delivery system laid on from the station to the store so there was no problem with the baggage.

On arrival Aunt Morag met them at the top of the stair. She seldom came down now as she found the stairs very difficult with her arthritis. However, she was fortunate as she had three very devoted domestics. After a few words of welcome they were sent off to wash as supper would be on the table in a few minutes. The boys, or the young men as they should more rightly be described, did full justice to the substantial meal which was set before them. Aunt Morag, although she had never been south of Inverness, was a very intelligent woman and a water colour artist. She specialised in highland scenes but always liked to include some live object, be it human or animal. Over the years she had sold quite a number of her pictures to visitors from the south. Both during supper and after, the exchange of family news continued. Reg found it difficult to take it all in but he did discover that his hosts only had two daughters, both married. One lived in the Moray Firth area and the other had emigrated to Canada with her husband.

Next morning, after a substantial breakfast, the two young men were taken on a tour of the store. It was a large building and they were amazed at the vast variety of goods on sale. There was fishing tackle, including waders, working men's clothes, shirts, trousers, even boots. There was ironmongery; everything from spades to saws, lamps, string, ropes, paraffin for lamps and goodness knows what besides. After this inspection the two young men took a walk round the town. In the south it would not have been described as a town but here it was a centre of importance. There was a hotel, a bank, a post office, and a butcher, a grocer, a baker and several small millinery shops. Then, of course, there were the Churches. Believe it or not this small community supported three. There was the Church of Scotland, the Free Kirk and the Roman Catholic Church. Ben gave Reg a brief history of the Churches in Scotland.

After a simple lunch they sat and chatted with Aunt Morag before being sent off to take a cup of tea with Aunt Cath. As they wandered up the road they came upon the blacksmith's shop. Here there was great activity; ponies were being shod and farm machinery repaired. Aunt Cath was a small, thin white-haired lady in her sixties. Her husband had been the bank manager but sadly died suddenly of a heart attack at the early age of fifty-two. They had three children, a son and two daughters. The son on leaving school had gone to Glasgow where he studied marine engineering. He was now second engineer officer on a large passenger liner. He had travelled all over the world. One daughter was married to a banker and lived in Thurso, the other to a farmer on the Black Isle. Aunt Cath was delighted to meet Ben as she had never met any of her brother Robert's family. She was interested to hear that they were going fishing and wished them luck. After their cup of tea they returned to the store.

That evening was spent receiving instructions on their journey tomorrow and a great deal of instruction on how to fish the hill lochs. Their journey on the morrow did not occasion an early start. Tom McCabe, the postman, could not leave until after the mail train had arrived and that was scheduled for ten thirty. Tom spent the early part of the morning going round several of the shops picking up standing orders for many of the homes on his round, then at about ten thirty he would report to the post office to pick up any mail for delivery and then set off. Today he had agreed that on leaving the post office he would call at the store as he would be passing the door anyway.

The two young men were sitting on the wooden seat outside the store when, soon after ten thirty, Tom drew up at the door. Tom jumped down and, approaching the two young men, said in his quiet spoken voice, 'Excuse me, but you two must be the two gentlemen who are to be accompanying me to Jock Bain the day.'

'Yes,' they replied and they shook hands. Tom having put their bags in the back of his vehicle climbed up and indicated that they should take their seats beside him, there was plenty of room on the wide bench seat. Meg, the garron pony, set off at a smart trot and on reaching the end of the houses they turned left up quite a small road. So far no words had passed between them.

Ben broke the silence by asking Tom, 'How far is it to Jock Bain's?'

'It would be about fifteen mile,' was the reply.

They were travelling through quite flat country with grass fields and one or two with a few drills of potatoes. They passed one family making hay then ahead they could see the road beginning to wind uphill. This brought Meg to a walk. After some fifteen minutes they crested the hill and they emerged out on to the open hill with heather down to the roadside. In about a mile the hill became steeper on either side and they entered a gorge in the bottom of which there was a considerable burn or small river. Their pace was now down to a walk; although the gradient was minimal the twists and corners were continuous. Slowly the sides of the ravine became less steep and they entered an area of birch trees. What a beautiful place, Reg thought, with rocks covered with blaeberries and bracken occupying the spaces between the trees. Few words passed between them but they were accompanied by the sound of Meg's hooves and the iron clad wheels on the gravel road. The gradient began to increase and Meg was obviously feeling it.

Tom suddenly said, 'I usually give the old girl a little help here,' and he jumped to the ground. The two lads followed and they all walked to the top of the ridge where they resumed their seats and followed the road down a slight incline to a burn which was spanned by a wooden bridge. Over the bridge there was a track which followed the burn up into the hills. They drew up beside what, to Reg, looked like a stone coffin or tank. Tom dismounted and lifted the smaller of the two slabs which formed the lid. He then took several packages from the cart and placed them under the fixed section and finally replaced the slab he had removed.

'Peg has been writing her letter again,' Tom said as he stuffed a letter and a penny into his pocket. 'I get one to post nearly every week. You will be wondering why they need such a hefty kist, well, I will tell you. It may be a day or two before they get down to collect their shopping and the foxes or pine martens could have them in that time.'

As they emerged from the little glen they left the trees behind them and the hill became less steep and more open. They plodded on with Meg breaking into a trot every now and again. It must have been some three miles further on, on rounding yet another corner, that they came in view of a house with several outbuildings.

As they drew up at the farm a lady appeared and said, 'I see you have company today, Tom, they will be fishermen going to stay with Jock, I'll be thinking.'

They climbed down and Tom explained that he always took his lunch with Jenny and Roy when he was at home. They followed Jenny into the kitchen with their lunch packets. They sat down at the table and Jenny produced mugs of tea. Jenny was a great talker and was soon putting the young lads through the mill. When she learnt that Ben was a nephew of Mr McKenzie she fairly went to town. 'I know him well, many a time he has sat where you are,' and so on. 'And the other young gentleman, where does he come from?' When she learnt that he came from the south of England he too had to go through her interrogation. After a happy forty-five minutes Tom declared it was time to move on.

In about twenty minutes they saw their objective some considerable distance ahead. When in a further ten minutes they finally arrived Peggy was waiting for them on the door step.

'There you are, lads, there's your home until I pick you up next week.'

'Come away in,' said Peggy, 'the kettle is on the hob.'

Tom then unloaded not only the suitcases but considerable quantities of stores. This done he called to Peggy, 'I will be on my way, see you next week, I have to make a call on my road home,' and off he went.

Peggy, leaving the fishing rods in the little front porch, showed the lads their room. It was small with two iron beds, a small chest of drawers with mirror on top and a washstand. There was no carpet, only a short runner between the beds. Having been shown the outside toilet they sat down in the kitchen for a chat.

Peggy started by saying, 'Mr McKenzie will have told you what to expect in our little home so I will leave it at that.' She went on to explain that they had no fixed time for meals except breakfast; that depended on when the fishers came home and when Jock came off the hill. The main meal would be in the evening, usually about six.

'What is Jock doing today?' Reg asked.

'Oh, he is over the hill helping Peter with some sheep, he'll not be home till tomorrow.'

After a little more chat Ben and Reg suggested that they would go for a walk and Peggy explained where the nearest lochs were.

What a wonderful start for their fishing holiday. It was a beautiful warm August day with just a few high clouds and a light west wind. They followed the pony path and in about fifteen minutes came in sight of the first loch. It was quite large, possibly three quarters of a mile long and half a mile wide. As they had plenty of time they decided to walk right round the loch. They had great fun planning how they would fish it tomorrow and in addition had quite a problem getting over the burn which ran into the top of the loch. In the end they removed their socks and shoes and waded through.

After a most exhilarating walk they arrived back to find Peggy coming in from the byre where she had been milking the cow. While Peggy prepared the meal they unpacked their fishing tackle. It was not long before Peggy came and announced, 'Your dinner is ready, gentlemen, when you are ready to take it.'

They packed up their things and went to the kitchen. There in the window was a small table with a white tablecloth and set with two places. As they sat down Reg could not help noticing Peggy. She was a nice looking girl, about five foot four, slim and about thirty years of age. She had taken the trouble to put on a tidy skirt and clean blouse and apron to serve them. As she did so she said, 'I hope you don't get bored with my cooking but it is difficult to produce variety up here. When you bring in some fish that will help.'

They assured her that they would never get bored with the delicious meal which they had enjoyed that evening.

'When do you eat, Peggy?' asked Ben. 'Why don't you join us?'

'No, Sir, I could not do that, it would not be right. I will eat later.'

'Where did you learn to become such a good cook?' asked Reg.

'I worked for six years in the big house before Jock and I got married,' she replied. They learnt that that had been seven years ago.

They finished their meal and left the room to allow Peggy to get finished up. They walked round to the back of the house where they found a range of buildings. On the end nearest to the house was a dog kennel, then an open door inside which they saw a stall for a pony, three ties for cows and a small pen suitable for calves. There followed a closed door which they took to be a dry goods store and finally on the other end a hen house to which a few hens were returning to roost. They walked on and over a small crest, and came upon a sheep fank and a corrugated roofed wooden shed. Some time later, having returned to the house, they were tidying up their room in the failing light when there was a knock at the door and Peggy invited them through for a cup of tea before going to bed. This time she agreed to join them. They had the most informative chat during which they learnt that Jock was an employed shepherd but was allowed to keep twenty ewes for himself and as many cows as he could feed through the winter. They slipped off to bed early, knowing that Peggy would be up early to milk the cows and prepare their breakfast.

At seven they were woken by Peggy's arrival with a large jug of hot water. Having washed and dressed they made their beds before reporting for breakfast. Breakfast consisted of porridge, a boiled egg and bread and butter. Before rising from the table they were presented with a small wooden lunch box. There was no paper for wrapping up sandwiches up there. As the weather looked doubtful they decided to take their coats and dump them at the lochside. Ben volunteered to carry the lunch box.

On arrival they found a nice sheltered bank under which they deposited all inessential items and prepared to start fishing. The plan was to fish together up one side and down the other. Ben, who was the more experienced fisherman, was to lead and Reg follow about one hundred yards behind. The lead would be changed every so often. By lunch time they had only caught three small fish, all of which they had put back. They put down their rods and walked back to see what the lunch box contained. Inside they found oat cakes and cheese and girdle scones filled with butter and the minimum of jam. As the rain had held off they did not hurry over their lunch but sat talking and enjoying the scenery.

The afternoon proved much more productive. Isn't it strange how often when fishing on a loch the fish will suddenly start taking and then just as suddenly stop? It was during one such period they caught seven keepable trout. They returned home about six, looking forward to presenting their catch to Peggy. Before reaching there, however, they saw two collie dogs approaching and almost immediately up walked a short well-built man wearing a deer-stalker hat. He greeted them with a huge smile and shook them by the hand. His only comment was, 'Have you got my tea with you?' Jock was obviously a great character and apologised for not being at home when they arrived. As they walked home, one behind the other on the narrow path, little passed between them.

On arriving at the house, Jock said to Reg, 'I will take those fish through to Peg and tell her that you are ready for your dinner.'

Peg served them their dinner, Jock did not even make an appearance. However, when it was time for the final cup of tea Jock was there. Conversation flowed during which they learnt that Jock had been two years in the place on his own before he got married. He explained that when he was alone he did not bother about the house, but put all his efforts into improving the croft. He had fenced in the paddock which enabled him to make hay which in turn enabled him to keep two cows and their calves. Once Peggy had appeared on the scene they had started on the house. As they rose to go to bed Jock said he was sorry he could not go to the lochs tomorrow as he must get on with his hay while the good weather lasted.

Next morning there was not a cloud in the sky and it looked like being a scorcher so Ben and Reg decided to abandon fishing and offered to help with the hay. This offer was willingly accepted and during the day not only did they get all that was cut turned and then raked up into coils but Jock got some fresh grass cut. Having worked hard all day they prevailed on Peggy to give them their dinner early so that they could go fishing once the sun was down. However, once they got there they found that there was not a breath of wind, the loch was a glassy calm and the midges were out in force. They were just about to pack it in when Reg, fishing where the main burn entered the loch, suddenly got into a fish. He was soon aware that this was something bigger than they had encountered so far. After much splashing and many anxious moments at last he netted a two and a half pound trout. Ben, not wishing to be left out, fished on for a time but in the end the midges won.

Saturday was just as hot as Friday so Ben and Reg said they would turn and make the hay which Jock had cut which would allow him to continue with his scythe. By mid-day all available grass was cut and all cut grass coiled up. While they were eating their lunch Jock said he must go and gather in a few ewes which had been missed at shearing and he asked if the young gentlemen would care to come with him and he could show them where the back lochs were, so that was the plan.

Having collected Meg and Laddie, the two collies, they set off past the fank. After about a mile Jock said he was going to cut out west and come up a ridge which they could see on their left. He asked the boys to follow the ridge in front and note any unclipped sheep they saw, saying that they could pick them up on their way home. They planned to meet at the high top. Ben and Reg could see a top not too far in front of them but they knew that was not their final objective, it was further on. When they reached the first ridge they discovered that there was a lot of ground between them and the high top including several intermediate ridges. As they climbed they came on one or two small bunches of sheep but these had all been clipped. Finally, on reaching what they were confident was the last intermediate top, they saw about a quarter of a mile away on their right two unclipped sheep with one lamb. The last bit of the climb was quite steep and they thought they had done well getting there so quickly when they noticed coming along the top on their left Jock with three ewes and two lambs. He soon reached them and asked what they had seen. They told him that they had seen two and they pointed in the direction where they had seen them.

Jock replied, 'That's fine, that's them all; I was only missing five.' Suddenly he called out, 'Meg go away by,' or something like that, and pointed in the direction where the sheep had been seen and off went Meg at top speed. Jock then turned to Ben and Reg and said, 'Would you two young gentlemen mind standing behind me, in fact you could have a seat if you wish, while I deal with these three.'

Ben and Reg had no idea what was to follow but they willingly sat down and watched. Jock took a pair of shears from his pocket and stuck them in the ground; he then said something to Laddie who moved to the far side of the sheep. Jock pointed at one of the ewes with his stick and said something further to Laddie who immediately started stalking in towards the ewe ever so slowly. The ewe turned to face the dog. This gave Jock his opportunity and quick as a flash he was in behind the ewe and caught her by the horns. He half carried her back to his shears and in a few minutes her fleece was off. Just at that moment the two remaining ewes with the one lamb appeared over the ridge on the east with Meg behind them. Before letting the shorn ewe go, Jock produced a small bottle from his pocket and put his mark in red paint on the off side of the beautiful white wool of the ewe.

In no time Meg's party had joined the little flock. 'Well done, Meg, that's a clever girl, sit down now.' It took Jock and his two dogs less than forty minutes to remove the fleeces of all five ewes. Jock laid the five fleeces on top of one another, rolled them up, secured them with a piece of string and slung them on his back.

'My goodness, those dogs are clever,' remarked Reg.

'Well you see, if I did not have the dogs I would have to take the ewes all the way home just for those few minutes and that is very hard on the lambs.'

They left the ewes on the hill and walked home. What a wonderful experience that had been.

Next day Jock, in return for all the help they had given with the hay, said he would take them to the back lochs. These lay just round the corner from where Jock had gone to find his ewes. They were quite small and had only about one hundred yards between them. The hill rose steeply behind them and it was obvious that, although small in area, they were deep. They decided that Reg would start on the top loch and Ben the bottom one and that after lunch they would change over. The morning yielded only three fish, all to Ben's rod.

The day's proceedings came to an earlier end than they had planned owing to a slight mishap to Reg. Having already caught two fish he thought he could save himself a detour by climbing along the steep rocks, after all, it was only a few yards. Unfortunately, he slipped and down into the loch he went. He was a good swimmer, but oh how cold the water was. Having clambered out he stripped off and squeezed as much water from his clothes as possible but in spite of that he decided he was too cold to continue. Ben, who had witnessed what had happened, decided to return home with him. The day had yielded seven fish in total.

At that moment Jock, who had wandered up the hill while the young gentlemen fished, reappeared. 'Jock, you take my rod and I will walk home,' said Reg, but Ben said, 'No, I have had enough, we will all go home.'

After walking for some time Reg's clothes began to dry and he warmed up. On arriving home Peg sent Reg to change saying, 'Bring your wet clothes to me and I will dry them in front of the fire.' When Reg went to bed that night he found on his bed his suit all nicely pressed and his underwear washed and folded.

On the Monday evening Jock said, 'Tomorrow I will take you to another loch. It is quite a way away but holds some good fish.' He explained that it was not on his beat but was part of the property.

Next morning off they set and after a walk of some five miles in a direction they had not been before they arrived at a beautiful loch about the same size as the home loch. With Jock to guide them there their efforts were more successful and they returned home with ten fish averaging over half a pound.

Before they knew where they were, Wednesday had come round and it was time to return home. When Reg asked what they owed for their holiday Peggy replied, 'Oh, nothing; Mr McKenzie has fixed all that. We only hope you have enjoyed your time in our little home.'

Reg, in his turn, said he had never enjoyed himself so much, it had been a perfect holiday.

At about three thirty Tom appeared with a considerable load of stores and it was time to shake hands and climb aboard. On the way down the two young men could not stop talking about what a wonderful time they had had, about the fishing, and the gathering of the lost ewes. The pony, with her head towards home, trotted out briskly. They stopped once or twice to pick up mail and other objects from boxes at road ends and once or twice at a cottage door. Tom being, as we have said, a man of few words, very little was said. It was after seven when they drew up outside the store. They asked Tom what they owed him for the round trip. 'Ach man,' he replied, 'Mr McKenzie fixed all that, in any case it is not often I have the pleasure of the company of two young gentlemen on my lonely journey.' They parted after warm handshakes and many words of thanks. Supper was waiting for them and what an evening they had telling of all that had happened during their week.

They had to be up early next morning to catch the train for Inverness and on to St Andrews. They left after many words of gratitude and regrets that their stay had come to an end. Aunt Morag presented them with a huge lunch box full of delicious sandwiches, scones and cakes. As they waited on the station platform everyone seemed to know Uncle Ben and they got chatting to four men who were on their way to Dingwall for the day. The train came in and the boys, having said good-bye to Uncle Ben, followed their companions into a third class compartment. Their new friends were all farmers on their way to a sale in Dingwall. During the next few minutes the young men were closely questioned on what they had been doing. During the course of their questioning it became obvious that Jock was quite well known as a dog handler and always competed in the local sheep dog trials. They were sorry to lose their companions at Dingwall. The remainder of the journey to St Andrews was uneventful and they were home in time for dinner.

Reg could not get over the generosity of Uncle Ben, he would not allow the boys to pay for anything.

Next morning Ben returned to Edinburgh to continue his studies and Reg got down to writing up his journal. On Saturday Reg declined an offer of a game of golf and contented himself with a long walk along the beach. After a quiet weekend during which he had several long discussions with his uncle, he returned home on Monday.

He found his parents in good form and anxious to hear all about his holiday. His parents had never heard of Uncle Ben and were greatly amused to hear all the details of his trip.

Reg took several long walks, visiting the various employees. On one occasion he came on the Baron out at grass with other horses. He wondered if he should have him sent over to Cambridge where he could keep him at livery.

Once back at Cambridge he decided that he did not think he would have enough time to justify bringing the Baron over. He spent more time participating in Union debates and as a result found himself on the management committee.

Through his many visits to farms he got to know several of the local land owners. It was from one of these, a certain Mr Williamson, that he received an invitation to shoot partridges. At lunch time he was questioned by some of the other guns about what he was reading and when they heard that it was agriculture he became even more acceptable, so much so that he received several other invitations to shoot.

Before he knew where he was it was time to return home for Christmas. Once home he had to organise his father's shoot, but what he really wanted to do was to have a day's hunting on the Baron. The opportunity came quite soon with a meet within hacking distance. He had been riding him in a double bridle and he had behaved well over the practice fences at home so he was confident that all would be well. At the meet several people complimented him on his new mount. It was some time before they found a fox and the field began to move off at some pace. The Baron behaved very well but when they approached the first fence he set off. Reg did not wish to check him in front of the fence so let him go and they flew over at a great pace. Reg soon learnt that his new horse was going to require careful riding and certainly could not be checked in front of a fence. What a wonderful day he had, with never a dull moment.

After a few days he began to build up quite a reputation as a flier and someone to follow if you wished a lead. He discussed with his groom the possibility of entering the Baron for the local point-to-point, who promised to have him fit for him when he returned at Easter. The shoot went well and soon it was time to return to Cambridge.

Once back there he wondered if he would bring the Baron over and keep him at livery and follow the local drag hunt. Once again he decided against doing so. If he did so he would either neglect his work and hunt all the time or if he did not it would not be worth the expense. A few days later he received an invitation from Uncle Sam Wilson for a day's shooting on Saturday and to stay the night. Having no horse at livery he readily accepted this kind invitation. When the time came, travelling by bicycle with a gun and cartridges was out of the question so he booked a cab.

He wrote to Uncle Sam accepting the invitation and setting out his proposed travelling plans.

It was not long before the date came round. He travelled up on Friday evening and it was wonderful to be sitting in front of the fire chatting to Uncle Sam. Uncle Sam explained that, not owning any shooting himself, he shared a rough shoot with a friend. He went on to explain that there probably would not be much to shoot but that he had invited one or two friends for dinner whom he thought Reg would enjoy meeting.

The next day was damp and looked as if it could rain at any moment. Fortunately, it held off and they had quite an enjoyable day with the four guns accounting for three brace of partridges, three cock pheasants, four hares and five pigeons.

It turned out that there were to be two other guests, both of whom would be staying the night. The other two were Sir Ronald Roper, a retired Indian Civil Servant, and a Mr Thomas Black, the local MP. Over a drink before dinner Uncle Sam explained to his guests that Reg was a scholar from Cambridge whom he had known for some years. The conversation before dinner was mostly about the day's shoot and other local matters. After dinner, as they sat round the dinner table with their glass of port, they discussed India and its future. At that time it was very much a very important part of the Empire. A future in such a wonderful venture sounded attractive to Reg. Discussion on the political situation at home followed. Both these subjects were more or less closed books to Reg and he realised what a lot he had to learn about life. Finally, they moved through to the study and the conversation became a lot less serious, mostly about local people and local gossip.

Next morning Reg raised the question of employment in the Indian Civil Service, and they discussed whether there was a place for an agriculturalist, such as he was, in India. Sir Ronald thought that there would be, but he was not sure. He promised to make some enquiries and let Reg know. Mr Black, wishing to keep his end up, asked Reg if he had ever thought of standing for Parliament. Reg replied that he had not, while he was still young he was thinking of something a little more adventurous than that.

They then all walked down to the local church, where Uncle Sam read the lesson. The little walk back ensured a good appetite for an excellent lunch. After lunch Reg left, having said a very warm thanks to Uncle Sam and obtained two new addresses for his journal.

About three weeks later Reg received a letter from Sir Ronald. He said that he had been unable to identify any specific jobs but he was sure there must be opportunities for someone with his qualifications. He gave the name and address of a contact in the India Office. Reg, having written to thank Sir Ronald, wrote to the contact in the India Office.

Reg on returning home found his parents well and the Baron in spanking form. A few days later, when out with the hounds, Reg was approached by a middle aged man who asked if he would be riding the Baron in the local point-to-point. Reg replied that he was not, as the Baron had been with a professional trainer and had run under National Hunt Rules, all of which ruled him out.

'Would you care to ride my horse then?' enquired his new friend. 'Poor old Paddy couldn't win but he is a safe jumper and they are always looking for entries.'

'But I have never ridden in a race, aren't you taking a risk asking a novice like me?'

'Well, I have admired the way you have flown over the country on that horse of yours.'

'Well,' replied Reg, 'I think it would be fun but could I have a ride on your horse before making a final decision?'

'Yes, of course, what about Friday morning?'

'I will ride over to your place about ten thirty.'

'I will expect you at our stable at that time.'

Sharp at ten thirty Mr Thorn rode into the stable yard. They quickly exchanged horses and set off. They went for a short hack round before returning to the field with the practice fences. Reg suggested to Mr Thorn that he should just watch as he did not wish him carried over into the lane as he had been. This agreed, Reg rode off. Paddy proved to be no slug, and jumped splendidly. On returning to Mr Thorn, Reg, smiling broadly, said, 'Yes I would love to ride him, I enjoyed that.' They agreed that on the day, which was still two weeks away, they would meet at the course at least an hour before the race was due to start. They exchanged horses and Mr Thorn set off for home.

At lunch Reg told his father what he had agreed to do. His father replied by saying, 'I shall have to make an effort to go to the races that day, I have not been for ages.'

When the day came Reg drove over with his father. They found Mr Thorn and everything seemed to be in order. When the time came a Steward led the competitors off to the start which was about half a mile out to the left. The course selected was in fact not a true point-to-point but out, round an isolated cottage and back. At the start some riders set off at a ridiculous pace and soon there were a number of fallers. Paddy jumped boldly and Reg soon found himself out with the leaders. By the time they approached the cottage Paddy was beginning to find the pace too hot. On rounding the cottage there was no obvious way straight home. A sharp turn led one into a corner from where there was no obvious way out. The leader kept looking left for a way through. Reg, knowing that now he had nothing to lose, turned right down into the corner. As he approached it he was convinced that if he was prepared to jump diagonally over two fences he could get through. He crammed on his hat and asked Paddy to have a go. True to form, he went straight out over the corner and they were through. He set off for home very much on his own. The others had found that they had had to go further round than they had expected. When they finally got round they saw Reg some two fields ahead of them. As they approached the winning post they were rapidly overhauling the leader but it was too late and Reg held on to win by about four lengths.

'How on earth did you manage to get so far ahead of us?' was fired at Reg.

'Oh, I just jumped out at the corner below the cottage,' Reg replied.

'I never thought one could get through there.'

Mr Thorn came up shaking with laughter and full of congratulations.

'If he had not been such a bold horse I could never have done it, he jumped out of that corner below the cottage like a lion.'

Reg's father came up full of praise and soon he was surrounded by quite a crowd of admirers. The news of his success filtered round the local hunts and in about two weeks he received a letter of congratulations from Felicity. In her letter she invited him to stay. Reg, in his reply, explained that the Easter vacation was too short but hoped for another invitation.

Back at Cambridge, knowing that there would be exams, Reg curtailed his social and other activities. He did however, lay on a weekend visit to the Smiths at Newmarket. He planned to go up by coach on Friday afternoon and return by the early one on Monday morning. When the weekend came he received a wonderful welcome not only from the Smiths but from all the staff. That evening was spent catching up with one another's news. The Smiths were much amused by the story of his point-to-point success.

'What about you riding out with the early string tomorrow? If you would like that I will fix up a mount for you.'

Reg, of course, jumped at the idea. Next morning as the string proceeded up the heath Reg rode up the line chatting to each lad in turn. There were one or two new lads who did not know him to whom he had to introduce himself. When they got back to the yard he had difficulty escaping for his breakfast.

Reg had deliberately selected a weekend when he knew there was a local race meeting. He got to the races by riding what otherwise would have been a led horse. It must have been at the second race, he was standing at the paddock when he felt a tap on his shoulder. Turning round there was General Isy.

'Hello, back at the races again?'

'Yes, just for one day,' Reg replied.

'It must have been almost a year ago that we met at dinner.'

'That's right, Sir, it was ten months ago.' They chatted on for a few minutes.

The afternoon went well and Bob had one winner and a second, the horse which Reg had ridden over. Reg rode him home again and handed him over to his lad. As he emerged from his box there was a Minister of Religion standing at the door of the box.

'Hello,' he said to Reg, 'I don't think we have met before. Are you the owner of this horse?'

'Oh no!' Reg replied, 'I have only ridden him back from the races, in fact I took a lift that way.' And Reg then had to explain the full circumstances of his presence. It was obvious to the Vicar that he was talking to a very intelligent young man.

'Would you care to come and have supper with us?' he asked

Reg. 'I don't think Mr and Mrs Smith would mind. Let's go and ask them.'

As they walked over the yard they ran into Bob. 'That will be all right, Vicar, I will tell him how to find you.'

It was a lovely warm evening as Reg sauntered over to the vicarage. The Vicar, a tall rather distinguished looking man, opened the door himself, standing behind him was his wife, a tall woman with grey hair. They were both probably in their fifties. Once inside, the Vicar, whose name was Browning, said, 'I do hope you do not mind my pinching you from the Smiths but we have not been here very long, just some two years, and we find it difficult to find well educated persons to socialise with. We love the stable lads, they are great fun, but their range of conversation is limited.'

Reg soon discovered that the Rev Browning had spent most of his life in Norwich with various Cathedral appointments. Another thing which had concentrated their attention on ecclesiastic matters was that they were childless. Mrs Browning gave Reg a very warm welcome, saying what a pleasant surprise it was for them to welcome him. 'We don't expect to find new friends in a stable yard.' The evening went by very quickly with the Brownings questioning Reg on his family background and then learning of his many sporting interests. Finally, they got round to Cambridge and what he was doing there. They were amazed to learn that he was a scholar and working to get an Honours degree. Reg found it difficult to question the Brownings in the same detail but learnt that they had spent most of their lives in Norwich. It was still quite early when Reg departed, promising to attend morning service on the morrow. Next morning, Mrs Smith agreed to accompany Reg to Church but Bob declined saying that he had too much to do.

After the service, while they were chatting to the Brownings, Rev Browning said to Reg, 'You remember you said last night that you had not decided on a career, well, have you thought of ordination? The Church could do with some bright young men like you.'

'No,' replied Reg.

'Well, think it over and if I can be of any help don't hesitate to ask.'

That afternoon he spent in the yard with Bob and the evening exchanging news with them both.

As he sat in the coach next morning the word ordination came into his mind and he spent some time turning over in his head what it would mean. No, he thought, I am not attracted to that idea, and by the time he had got back to college he had forgotten about it. He had enjoyed his break and set to his studies with renewed energy.

There was one thing he did do and that was to write to the India Office and make a date for interview at the end of term. That done he booked into the Plumbs for a couple of nights covering that period.

Some weeks later, with his exams behind him, he took the train to London. On arrival he was informed by Peter that he was to form part of a party for the following evening. Susan, Peter's eldest sister, had just come out and wished to entertain one or two friends. The party was to be at a fashionable hotel where they could dine and dance afterwards.

Next day, Reg had a very satisfactory interview at the India Office. He learnt that they could guarantee him a job but that the grading would depend on his final Cambridge Exam results. Whatever the job he would have to spend some months in London learning the ropes before going to India. It was left with the understanding that Reg would contact the India Office as soon as he knew his final results.

Later that evening at the party he found himself sitting next to a small rather dumpy little girl but one who was obviously very bright. They got on very well at dinner and later that evening when they were dancing together she asked him what he was going to do on coming down from Cambridge, with all that knowledge of farming and forestry. He explained that he was planning to join the Indian Civil Service and they chatted on about India. He was very taken with Silvia Birch and they exchanged addresses.

Next morning, he took the train for home without having made any positive plans for his summer holidays. Once home he found several letters waiting for him which included three invitations. There was one from Felicity inviting him to the cricket week-end, the second was from David Sells inviting him for the York Autumn Meeting and the third was from Sam Wilson asking him to go North with him. None of them clashed but they demanded a lot of travelling and was it fair to leave his parents so much? After discussion it was decided that he should accept them all. This left only the gaps at home. His studies at Cambridge had given him a number of questions and experiments he wished to discuss with his father and in particular, with Ken Oliver. Ken, being quite young, was prepared to make changes, in fact, he enjoyed the challenge and the opportunity to be the leader in the local agricultural field.

Before Reg knew where he was it was time to set off west and to see Felicity again. This time he had been invited three days before the cricket weekend. He received a great welcome from his cabbie friend at the station. On arrival at the house he received another great welcome from all the family and staff. The children had all grown tremendously but the biggest difference was in Felicity. She was now a real young lady, just as attractive, perhaps even more so. As it was a very warm day they sat outside and the younger members filtered away to play. In a few minutes, Sir Richard, who had not been present when Reg arrived, walked up the garden path and joined the party. Reg tried to steer the conversation to local news but was outnumbered and had to give way to answering a battery of questions. Eventually, Felicity came to the rescue by taking him away to see the horses. As they wandered down the path she said, 'I invited you two days early to accompany me tomorrow night to a large dinner party, I hope you don't mind,' and she proceeded to describe it. Reg was, of course, quite delighted that he had been selected for this duty.

What a happy evening they had with the next eldest of the children after dinner.

Next morning, Sir Richard took charge of Reg. After they had inspected the blood stock, which took considerable time, they returned to the house where Sir Richard, knowing that Reg was reading agriculture, questioned him on all sorts of farming and estate management problems. The afternoon was spent playing games with the children which included Lady Dart. Felicity and Reg were the only ones invited to the dinner party as it was primarily for their age group. On arrival they were ushered into a large hall where they were introduced to their host and hostess. Reg recognised a few faces from the dance he had attended when last staying with the Darts. The evening turned out to be rather a dull one with very little opportunity to meet new people.

Next day was the cricket match. On this occasion, Sir Richard won the toss and elected to bat. Runs came very slowly and the score was only 45 when Reg came in. The bowler was a fast one and Reg just nicked the ball which shot off behind. He looked to his partner for a call but nothing came so he looked round to watch the ball. He saw it obviously not going to reach the boundary when suddenly a dog shot out from the crowd, picked up the ball and returned to his place. Immediately the umpire signalled a boundary. The ball having been recovered the game continued. The next ball he managed to hit between two fielders and calling to his partner started to run. As his partner never moved he started to return to his crease, but was too late and was run out. He learnt later that his partner was not only deaf but of low intelligence. On this occasion, Sir Richard's team were badly beaten but everyone enjoyed themselves. Reg left for home on Monday with an invitation to return for a day with the hounds about Christmas time.

Soon after his return he received a surprise letter from David which contained even more surprising news. David revealed that he had invited Mary McKenzie to come up for the York Meeting. Reg did not know that David and Mary had kept in touch since the occasion of the charity ball in Edinburgh. The plan was for them to meet at the station and travel on the same train. This would necessitate only one carriage to meet them at York.

The days soon passed and it was time to set off again. He had no difficulty finding his cousin at the station and they settled down for a happy period catching up with one another's news.

Reg opened with, 'You are a dark horse, Mary, I had no idea you were corresponding, far less going out with David.'

Mary, blushing slightly, replied, 'Why shouldn't I?'

'No reason at all,' said Reg, 'I am delighted.'

They had so much to talk about that soon they found themselves at their destination. They were met by the same coachman as had met Reg on his previous visits. During the drive Mary said she was nervous, she had never been to a party of this nature. Reg reassured her and soon they were at the lodge. They were ushered into the drawing room where they found Lady Sells and Caroline.

Caroline welcomed Mary, saying, 'We are thrilled to meet you; you are the first girl that David has ever invited to stay.'

Caroline who was not one of the world's most beautiful girls although she was one of the nicest, was quite taken aback by the appearance of this tall beautiful girl from Scotland. It was not long, however, before the ice was broken and conversation was flowing freely. Lady Sells explained David's absence by telling them that a big ball was to be given by his grandparents and that he had to take charge. David, not being happy with so much responsibility, had taken his father with him. The three ladies and Reg chattered on for some time before Lady Sells suggested to Mary that perhaps she would like to rest after her long journey, so she went upstairs.

The ball was supposed to be held to celebrate David's twenty-first birthday but in addition only Lord and Lady Sells knew that David intended to announce his engagement to Mary during the evening. He had made this fact known to his parents about ten days before. His father, on hearing this, thought it would be nice if they could bring some Scottish element into the celebrations. It just so happened that a battalion of the Gordon Highlanders, commanded by an old friend, was stationed at Catterick, not too far away. He was delighted to co-operate and the following programme was put together: throughout the evening the Regimental Pipe and Brass Bands would be available. The party would start with a large family dinner party in the big hall. As ball guests arrived they would be entertained elsewhere until the dinner was over. Once dinner was over all guests would assemble outside where the two bands would play. This would allow the great hall to be cleared for dancing. All guests would then be assembled in the great hall and would be called to silence by a bugler and David's grandfather would announce the engagement of his grandson to Mary McKenzie.

Reg spent that evening catching up with all the happenings since he was last at the Lodge. Next morning David, Reg, Caroline and Mary went off to the races together with strict instructions not to be late back because of the ball that night. They had a most enjoyable day and according to instructions returned home in good time. The house seemed to be buzzing with activity as several more guests for the ball had arrived. When they assembled for the short journey the ladies were all wearing their coats so it was not possible to see what they were wearing. Carriages ran a shuttle service over to the dance. Here the ladies went to take off their coats while the gentlemen waited in the drawing room. When the ladies did appear Mary was walking with Lady Sells. She was dressed in a high waisted cream white ball gown with a silk McKenzie tartan plaid on her shoulder. She certainly made a very striking figure. They then all filed through to be introduced to their host and hostess.

When dinner was announced they moved through, led by the Earl and Countess. At dinner the small party from the lodge were spaced between the house guests. Reg found himself sitting between two ladies considerably older than himself. However, they both proved to be good conversationalists and Reg, who was rarely caught without something to say, got on very well with them both. Reg asked them if they knew Miss Brough and Miss Long. 'Of course we do,' they replied, 'everyone knows them.' Reg then described how he had met them on the train from York and what a fascinating journey he had had hearing all about their travels.

After a delicious dinner they went through and joined the ball guests. Almost immediately, everybody moved outside to hear and watch the bands play. It was a glorious evening and the pipe band marched back and forth while the brass band played from a platform. When the music finished the company assembled in the great hall from which all trace of dinner had been removed. The Earl mounted the platform and once silence had been established, welcomed everyone. He then congratulated David on achieving his majority and invited him to come up onto the platform where he shook his hand. This done he continued, 'I now have an even greater pleasure in announcing David's engagement to a most charming lady.' At this point Lord Sells conducted Mary onto the platform and his Lordship introduced her, 'Miss Mary McKenzie from St Andrews in Scotland,' whereupon a great cheer went up. At this point Lord Sells took over and announced, 'In a tribute to our Scottish guest a demonstration of Scottish highland dancing will be given by members of the Gordon Highlanders. Please clear the centre of the hall.'

This done, sixteen Highlanders accompanied by a single piper marched in. In the darkness on the lawn it had not been possible to see the full dress kilts of the bandsmen, as that is who this group were, now in the bright light they made a wonderful spectacle. Some of the girls noticed that they had replaced their heavy army boots with lightweight dancing pumps. They proceeded to dance a sixteensome reel followed by a foursome reel. Everybody was amazed at the standard of their dancing and the lightness and speed of their footwork. Another great cheer went up as they marched out. Lord Sells then announced, 'There will now be an interval during which you may congratulate the young couple after which the dancing will begin.' Reg soon had a full programme which included one dance with Mary.

Next day at the races everyone was talking about the wonderful ball and the beautiful girl from Scotland that David had got engaged to. After the exertions of the previous evening and a long day at the races everyone was ready for an early evening and Reg, knowing that he only had a few days before going north to Scotland, caught the train for home. He broke the news of Mary's engagement both to the Plumbs and to his parents. His mother, although obviously delighted, could not help showing a little jealousy that her niece had done so much better than her own daughter.

There was so much to do on the estate that the few days before he set off again soon sped by. When he had visited the horses out at grass he found the Baron looking very fat and well. Reg was looking forward to getting back in the saddle. Of course he had visited Ken Oliver and had long talks with him as to how things were going on the farm. Now it was time to set off again. He met Uncle Sam in London. This time, as he had done the journey before it went much quicker and of course he had plenty to talk about with Uncle Sam. When they arrived in Fort William it was pouring with rain. 'This will help the fishing,' remarked Uncle Sam. The drive home was very wet but what did that matter if it brought the fish up? They both received a great reception from all the family which on this occasion included all four children.

By after lunch the rain had stopped and Mrs Wilson went off to the river. She returned before dinner saying that the river was falling again and without success. Not long afterwards Mr Wilson returned having had a blank day on the hill.

The next day Uncle Sam went to the hill and the rest of the family amused themselves either flogging the river or playing games with the younger children. The day after that Reg was to go to the hill and the two elder girls asked him if they could go with him, this time properly shod with suitable footwear, so Reg set off accompanied by the two girls. It turned into a very hot day with very little wind. This meant that all the deer were very high up which in its turn meant a long walk to the top for the stalking party. Eventually, the top was reached after several stops and much cursing at the flies which plagued them. By this time it was lunch time. The girls enjoyed the achievement of getting to the top, and the little bit of breeze which helped to keep the flies away.

After lunch the stalker told the young people to enjoy the sunshine while he went and had a little look round the corner. He returned some fifteen minutes later and reported that he had only seen one bunch of stags, away west along the top. They were in a difficult place but never mind, fortune favours the bold. They set off slightly below the top to avoid being seen on the sky-line. The girls were thrilled, the walking was easy and the flies had gone. They walked for quite a long time before they stopped to have a look and try to pinpoint the exact position of the deer. They moved on again, this time quite a short distance and came to a stop behind a steep little bank. The stalker had a quick look. He said that they were still too far away for a shot but that the girls and the gillies should wait here and that he and Mr Reg would try and get nearer and off they went.

Once they had gone the girls asked the gillies if they could have a look. After being told of the danger of being seen on the sky-line they decided not to. They chatted to the gillies for some time and then closed their eyes and dozed off. Reg and the stalker walked forward behind the bank but when they next started to have a look they suddenly saw a young stag lying some ten or fifteen feet above the main bunch who had a commanding view in their direction. They sat down and waited, hoping that he might move or at least turn round and face the other way. They soon decided that this was unlikely to happen and that they must find some other way. They looked this way and that way and eventually decided that they would have to risk an open crawl. They started ever so slowly keeping a close watch on the young stag's head. Every time he moved his head they stopped until they thought he was asleep again. Suddenly, he got up but he did not look in their direction, instead he had a scratch, shook himself and stood gazing into space. Reg, who was in a very uncomfortable position, thought his neck would break if he had to keep his head up much longer but he dared not put it down as then he would not see what was happening. When he was just about to look away the young stag turned round, scraped the ground with his foot and lay down again. This time he was not facing so directly towards them.

With great relief they started their crawl again. They crawled forward like this for some time until, at last, they reached cover behind a little bank. After a moment's rest the stalker peeped round the corner and then quickly pulled the rifle from its cover and said, 'Follow me.' When Reg got round the corner he could see no deer and the stalker started to run. They soon made the next bank but there was no sign of deer. They moved forward until they could see the ground ahead and there were the deer some eight hundred yards ahead and still going away. The stalker, having had a quick look with his glass, turned to Reg and said, 'I thought we had made it, I wonder what put them off. Oh well, better luck next time.'

They stretched their limbs and walked back to find the others.

The girls said, 'What a long time you have been, what have you been doing?'

There followed a long explanation before they started the long walk home. At dinner that night the girls said how much they had enjoyed the day but how sad it was that no shot was fired. Next day, Reg was sent up again, this time he went alone. They got a stag quite early and Reg was home in time to have a go at the river. Owing to the low level of the river there was little chance of a fish but as it was Saturday and he had to leave for home on Monday he decided that he must try. On Monday he started his homeward journey alone as Uncle Sam was staying on for some time longer.

Soon after Reg's return his mother asked him if he would like a party for his twenty-first birthday which was due in February. After discussion it was decided that all he would like was a dinner party at home during the Easter vacation. After a relatively short period at home it was time for him to return to Cambridge. He worked hard as he was keen to get a good result. He did, however, find time to attend one or two partridge shoots with some of the kind people he had met the previous season. One thing he did do was to participate regularly in the Union debates. He considered that proficiency in public speaking would always stand him in good stead. Shortly before the end of term he received a letter from Felicity inviting him for a long weekend hunting and saying that they would mount him to save him bringing a horse.

On arriving home for Christmas he learnt that Arthur was expected home for Christmas. His mother immediately decided that they should organise a dance at the time of the annual shoot. In making up the invitation list she had a problem as she had no idea what the position of Arthur's engagement was. In his recent letters he had made no mention of his fiancée. In the end she decided to send her an invitation hoping that if things had gone wrong she would just refuse. In the meantime Reg had two most enjoyable days hunting on the Baron. It was just before he left that a letter arrived from Felicity telling him that on this occasion there was no dance involved and that he need not bring his tail-coat.

On arrival he found the same cabbie at the station; they were getting to know one another quite well. He received a great welcome from all the family; it was almost like coming home. During the evening Felicity told him that on the morrow he was to ride the very horse he nearly bought last year. The next day was very windy and a poor scenting day with the result that he and Felicity spent much time together chatting.

The weather remained very stormy on Sunday but by Monday morning it had settled down considerably. He spent a very happy Sunday playing with the younger children and chatting with his host and hostess.

They had quite a long hack-on on Monday morning and it was still quite blowy as they rode into the wind. The meet was at a large house where he had not been before. There were lots of trees round the house which gave good shelter and the first draw was these woodlands. Hounds spoke almost immediately and hunted round and round the house, then suddenly there was a hollo. Everybody dashed off in all directions down a variety of driveways and rides through the wood. Nobody seemed to know which way the hounds had gone. When Reg and his little group emerged into the open they could hear hounds away in the distance and they set off after them. In no time they came over a small crest and there were hounds which were casting about trying to pick up the line. They made nothing of it and they moved off to a fresh draw. It proved to be one of those unsatisfactory poor scenting days. They found another fox but once more soon ran out of scent. As they were getting further and further from home they decided to call it a day and start the long hack home.

Once home, Reg lay long in his bath wondering, am I falling in love with Felicity? She is a lovely girl and I am very fond of her, but does that mean falling in love? I don't wish to get married yet, I am enjoying the life I live. No, I am much too young and I love my freedom,' and he sprang from the bath.

The cold wind had taken its toll and everybody was very sleepy at dinner and ready for an early night. He and Felicity, as he had invited her to the home-coming party, arrived home next afternoon to find great activity. But the thing which was worrying his mother most was a telegram from Arthur stating that he and Mary would arrive by lunch time on the following day, but there was still no word from the first girl friend. Next morning the letter came. It was full of apologies for being so slow and saying she was looking forward to seeing Arthur again. It was not long before Arthur himself arrived accompanied by a tall rather austere-looking woman. They dispersed to find their rooms. Arthur was the first to reappear and his mother confronted him with THE letter. After a few words of explanation by his mother as to why Victoria was invited there followed a long silence. It was finally broken by his mother saying, 'Well, think it over and tell me what you are going to do.'

Arthur had met Mary in South Africa where she had been nursing and they had travelled home on the same boat. Arthur did not know what to do, so he decided to do nothing and try and ride it out. When Mary arrived down there were others in the room so he could not tell her what had happened. Later that evening when he did, Mary was very upset as she had no idea that Arthur had been engaged earlier. Just at that moment Victoria, the original girl friend, entered the room and seeing Arthur ran up to him and giving him a kiss, said, 'Oh Arthur, how wonderful to see you again. I was beginning to think you had forgotten all about me.'

Covered in confusion Arthur stepped back and said, 'This is Mary, we came home on the same boat.'

At that moment dinner was announced and Arthur moved off with Mary. Reg, seeing Victoria left stranded, rushed in to rescue her. Reg was accompanied by Felicity who could not understand what was going on. Victoria stood, head in hands, sobbing, 'He never told me there was another girl. I can't go in to dinner, I just want to go home.'

Reg said, 'I understand, let's go up to your room and we will work something out there.' Turning to Felicity he said, 'You go in. I will join you in a few minutes.'

Reg took Victoria by the arm and they left the room. Once back in her room she broke down and falling on Reg's shoulder burst into a flood of tears. Reg sat her on a chair and rang the bell. When the maid arrived he asked her to fetch his mother's lady's maid. When Mary D arrived Reg explained everything to her and left saying he would get his mother to come up as soon as possible. Reg rushed downstairs, whispered in his mother's ear what had happened and what he had arranged and went and joined Felicity.

In the main dining room there was one very large table which seated some thirty-six people. In addition there was a smaller table seating twelve. The Colonel and his wife Ethel sat at one end of the big table and Arthur and Mary at the other end. Reg and Felicity acted as hosts at the smaller table. The atmosphere in the dining room when Reg returned was gloomy in the extreme, few people spoke and those that did so did so almost in a whisper. The meal proceeded apace and it was not long before they reached the dessert. At this point the hostess slipped away to see what was going on upstairs and the Colonel announced that the dance would begin in fifteen minutes. This greatly relieved the tension and the atmosphere became more relaxed. In the meantime Arthur and Mary were having a difficult time. A few of Arthur's old friends tried to converse with him and Mary but found it very difficult as Mary would not move a foot from his side. Mary was very conscious of the antagonism felt towards her by almost everyone in the room.

Upstairs, Ethel found Victoria much more composed. She apologised to her for making such a terrible mistake but said that she herself had no idea of Mary's existence. The two ladies chatted together for some time during which they planned Victoria's departure next morning. Downstairs the Colonel announced at quite an early hour that the next dance would be the last one. As soon as it was over people were quick to take their leave and those staying in the house slipped off to bed. In a moment there was only the Colonel and his two sons. Arthur announced that he and Mary would be leaving next morning for London as he must buy some new clothes, after which they all three retired to bed.

Next morning, Reg was down early in case he could be of some help to his parents. Before he had finished his breakfast his father arrived. 'What a shambles that was last night,' he said. 'We will now have to see what we have to do to sort it out. Your mother has gone to see Victoria and say good-bye to her before she slips away. I was very sorry for her last night; it must have been a terrible shock to her to find Arthur with that other woman, especially when we invited her to the party.'

It was not long before one or two other guests appeared, no mention of the proceedings of the evening was made by anyone. It was quite late before Arthur appeared accompanied by Mary. He announced that as soon as they had had their breakfast they would be leaving for London to do some essential shopping after such a long time out of the country. Reg suggested to Felicity that, as it was such a lovely morning, he would drive her to the station in the pony trap. This he knew would give them an opportunity for a private chat. Felicity expressed her sympathy for Reg's parents for whom the whole thing must have been a great embarrassment, and so ended one of the most disastrous parties ever held at Wantock.

Epilogue

It was almost time for Reg to return to Cambridge when he received a letter from the general manager of the Duke of Fever Estates asking him if he, on completion of his studies at Cambridge, would consider joining the estate management team. If he was interested could he come for interview on one of the following dates and three alternative dates were given. The interviews would be held in London at the Duke's London house. As he was still at home he discussed the offer with his father and they both thought it was worth following up, so he wrote saying that he would come for interview on one of the suggested dates.

He returned to Cambridge and renewed his studies with energy. The date that Reg had selected was just before Easter and when he arrived he found that he was the only candidate. It was explained to him that too many of the estate activities were out of date and that they wished to make a review of the whole estate and then draw up an improvement plan. He realised that this was a great challenge and when he heard the financial rewards he could not resist accepting should he be offered the position. He was offered the job, which he accepted. He returned to Cambridge where he sat his final exams. As was not unexpected, he got a first class honours degree.